Locker 217

José F. Nodar

Camden Books Publishing

Locker 217 / José F. Nodar
ISBN: 978-1-7644759-4-5 - Paperback
ISBN: 978-1-7644759-5-2 - E-Book

Dedication

In loving memory of my wife,
Miriam Vassallo Nodar,
and her enduring presence.
You are always in my thoughts.
For anyone who's ever loved deeply, lost fully, and still found
the courage to begin again.

Table of Contents

CHAPTER 1

The Locker Mishap

I used to think Tuesdays were invisible days, not bad like Mondays, not exciting like Fridays, just... there.

Like the colour beige.

Or the sound the fridge makes when no one's listening.

Tuesdays rarely happen to you. You just moved through them quietly and hoped no one noticed your shoelaces were uneven or that you still couldn't open your locker without wrestling it like an angry metal octopus.

That Tuesday started exactly like that.

Invisible.

Which is how I know the universe was planning something.

I was standing in the Year Four corridor, which smelled like old banana peels and floor cleaner that pretended to be lemon but absolutely wasn't. The bell had rung three minutes ago, which meant I was already late, which meant Mrs Calder would do that thing where she raised one eyebrow and sighed like I had shortened her life.

My locker, number 217, stared back at me with its scratched blue door and a dent near the handle. We had a history, that locker and me.

Bad history.

I twisted the dial carefully. Right to twenty-two. Left to nine. Right to—*Click.*

No, no, no, that wasn't a good click.

That was a *fake* click.

The one that meant the locker had decided today was not my day.

I sighed dramatically, because if you're going to suffer, you might as well suffer properly.

Behind me, Sam, my little brother, bounced on his heels.

"Leo," he said, tugging at my sleeve. "Did you know Jupiter is so big you could fit all the other planets inside it and still have room for, like, a million Earths?"

"That's not true," I muttered, twisting the dial again.

"It is *mostly* true," Sam said cheerfully. "Mr Henson said so. Also, Jupiter has a giant red storm that's been going for three hundred years and—"

"Sam," I said through my teeth, "I am trying to unlock my *locker.*"

He went quiet.

Which meant he was still talking in his head.

Sam was seven and believed facts were shared immediately, like emergencies. Especially space facts. He wore the same galaxy hoodie three days a week and had once cried because Pluto wasn't a planet anymore.

I looked at the dial one more time and tried again.

Right. Left. Right. Nothing.

A group of kids walked past us—Ethan Clarke and his friends, laughing loudly, backpacks swinging as if they owned the place.

Ethan glanced at me. Not directly. Just enough to know that he had noticed. My ears burned.

I suddenly noticed how I was standing.

Of how long I'd been at my locker.

Of Sam hopping from foot to foot behind me like an excited puppy.

Social standing is a weird thing.

You don't care about it at all until one day you wake up and realise you care about it *a lot*, and you don't remember agreeing to that.

I leaned closer to the lock, squinting as if that would help.

"Come on," I whispered. "Don't do this to me."

That's when it happened.

The locker door shuddered—not open, not closed, just enough to release a single folded piece of paper.

Pink, definitely pink.

It fluttered down in slow motion, like something important does in movies.

I watched it fall, and I didn't breathe and it landed right at my feet.

Before my brain could catch up, Sam stepped forward and *planted his shoe on it.*

"Sam!" I hissed.

He froze. Looked down. Looked up at me.

"What?" he asked innocently. "I thought it was rubbish."

"That is *not* rubbish." I said.

"How do you know?" he asked.

Because rubbish isn't folded neatly into a square. Because rubbish isn't pink. Because rubbish doesn't appear mysteriously from a locker that hates you on an invisible Tuesday.

"Move," I said.

Sam lifted his foot. The paper stayed exactly where it was, as if glued to the floor by destiny or chewing gum.

I bent down slowly, my heart thumping so loudly I was pretty sure everyone could hear it. I picked it up. It was warm from Sam's shoe.

"Is it a note?" Sam asked, eyes wide.

I didn't answer. I just stared at it. I had never received a note before. I mean, I'd received *notes*—permission slips, reminders that my handwriting looked like a spider had fallen into ink and panicked—but not *a note*. Not the kind of people whispered about. The kind that could change things.

"Are you gonna read it?" Sam whispered, even though the corridor was nearly empty now.

"Not here," I blurted.

"What if it's from a secret admirer?" he said.

I snorted. "No one admires me."

"That's not true," Sam said. "Mum admires you."

"That doesn't count."

I shoved the pink square into my pocket just as Mrs Calder's voice echoed down the corridor.

"Leo Marshall. Sam Marshall. Why are you still here?"

"We're coming!" Sam called.

I yanked my locker open at last—of course it chose *that* moment—grabbed my books, and hurried after Sam, my pocket feeling suddenly heavier than it should.

Throughout math, I couldn't concentrate.

Numbers floated on the page, meaningless. Mrs Calder explained fractions, but all I could think about was the folded paper pressing against my leg. It felt like it was buzzing. Or maybe that was my imagination.

Who wrote it? Why was it in *my* locker? And most importantly—what did it say?

At recess, Sam followed me straight to the far end of the oval, near the old fig tree where the bark peeled as if it had sunburn.

"Can I see it?" he asked.

"No."

"Why not?"

"Because it's private."

"What does private mean?"

"It means you don't get to see it."

He frowned. "But I helped find it."

"You stepped on it."

"Which kept it safe," he said proudly.

I sighed. "Fine. But you can't tell anyone. Anyone."

He crossed his heart dramatically. "I swear on Jupiter."

I pulled the note out of my pocket. It was slightly creased now, not as perfect as before. My hands were sweaty. I unfolded it carefully.

Inside, written in neat, curly handwriting, were just four words.

Meet me after school.

That was it. No name. No smiley face. No explanation.

Sam leaned in so close his nose almost touched the paper.

"Ooooooh," he breathed. "That's mysterious."

My stomach flipped.

"Who do you think it is?" he asked.

"I don't know," I said, but my brain was already racing.

It couldn't be someone older. Could it? Older kids didn't write notes. They just... existed loudly and confidently and laughed at you.

Maybe it was a prank.

That thought hit hard.

Only one person would come up with such a prank. Ethan Clarke and his friends. Pink paper. Laughter waiting around the corner.

I folded the note again, more sharply this time.

"It's probably nothing," I said.

Sam tilted his head. "Then why are your ears red?"

"They're not."

"They are."

"They're not."

He grinned. "You care."

I glared at him. "You are not telling anyone."

"I wouldn't," he said. "But if you *die* mysteriously, can I have your Lego?"

"You're impossible."

The rest of the day crawled.

Every time someone looked at me, I wondered if it was them. Every laugh sounded suspicious. I caught myself standing straighter, fixing my hair, trying to look... different. Like someone who got notes.

After the last bell, my heart pounded so hard I thought it might escape.

"Where are you going?" Sam asked as we packed up.

"I—uh—library," I said.

He squinted. "You hate the library."

"I like it now."

"That's suspicious."

"Go wait by the gate," I said. "I'll meet you."

Sam's eyes widened. "Is it happening?"

"Nothing is happening."

But something was.

I strolled toward the lockers. The corridor was quiet now, footsteps echoing. I stopped near 217.

I waited and waited.

Just when I was about to laugh at myself and leave, someone stepped out from behind the stairwell.

My breath caught.

They held a pink piece of paper.

"Hi," they said.

And just like that, Tuesday stopped being invisible.

CHAPTER 2

The Person Behind The Paper

I had imagined a lot of possibilities while waiting. A prank, a dare, a teacher, or maybe a ghost.

I had *not* imagined her.

She stood there holding another pink note as if it were a shield, her fingers pinching the edge so tightly that it bent. She was from my year; I knew that much straight away, but not from my class. She wore her hair in two low plaits and had a freckle near her left eyebrow, like someone had flicked a bit of cinnamon at her and missed the rest of her face.

"Hi," she said again, quieter this time.

My brain completely stopped working.

This was unfortunate because my brain is usually the thing I rely on most.

It notices things; it fills in gaps; it narrates my life like a documentary with dramatic music. But right then, it had taken a holiday.

I stared, and she stared back.

Somewhere in the distance, a door slammed.

A pigeon flapped.

Time continued rudely without my permission.

"Hi," I finally managed, which was disappointing because I had planned something cooler.

She shifted her weight from one foot to the other.

"I wasn't sure if you'd come," she said.

"I wasn't sure if I would," I replied, which was true and also sounded mysterious, so that was good.

She smiled a little at that. Not a big smile, a careful one.

"I'm Mia," she said. "Mia Collins."

"Oh," I said. "I'm Leo."

She nodded. "I know."

Of course, she did.

Everyone knew my name.

That meant nothing.

It definitely didn't mean something important was happening.

"So," I said. "You wrote the note?"

She nodded again, this time more quickly, like she was worried I might change my mind.

"Sorry," she added. "If that was weird."

"It wasn't," I said immediately.

Too immediately. "I mean, it *was weird,* but not bad weird. Just unusually weird."

She laughed. A brief burst, like she hadn't meant to.

"I didn't know how else to do it," she said. "I couldn't just come up to you. Everyone's always around."

I thought of Sam, of Ethan, of corridors full of watching eyes.

"Yeah," I said. "I get that."

We stood there again, both of us clearly waiting for the other to say the next thing. It felt like one of those moments in video games where the characters freeze until you press a button.

"So," I said, because apparently that was my word now. "Why did you want to meet me?"

She looked down at the pink paper in her hands. Folded it. Unfolded it.

"I saw what you did," she said.

My stomach dropped.

"What did I do?"

"Last Thursday," she said. "At lunch."

My brain scrambled backward through time. Thursday. Lunch. I had eaten a squashed sandwich and tried not to get hit by a football.

"I did nothing," I said cautiously.

"You did," she said. "You gave your apple to that kid."

"Oh," I said.

That kid was Noah Patel. He was in Year Three and cried easily and had once told me his dad worked night shifts and forgot to pack his lunch sometimes. I had an apple. He hadn't. It hadn't seemed like a big deal.

"He looked like he needed it," I said.

She nodded. "Most people just pretend not to notice."

I shrugged, suddenly very aware of my hands and what they were doing, which was nothing useful.

"It was just an apple."

"Still," she said. "I noticed."

My goodness, that word again.

Noticed.

Something warm and uncomfortable spread through my chest.

"Okay," I said. "But that doesn't explain the note."

She hesitated.

"I need help," she said.

That definitely wasn't what I was expecting.

"Help with what?" I asked.

She glanced around the corridor, even though we were alone.

"With something important," she said. "And you're good at noticing things."

I almost laughed.

Not because it was funny, but because it felt strange hearing something I'd always known quietly in my head said out loud by someone else.

"How do you know that?" I asked.

She smiled again, a little bigger this time.

"You always look," she said. "Everyone else just walks. You look."

I swallowed.

This was officially the weirdest and most important conversation I had ever had.

"What kind of help?" I asked.

She took a breath.

"There's a note," she said.

I blinked. "A note?"

"Yes," she said. "Another one."

I stared at her.

"You wrote me a note... about a note?"

"No," she blurted. "I didn't write *that* one."

My heart did a strange little jump.

"Then who did?"

"That's the problem," she said.

She held the pink paper in her hands. "Can you walk with me?"

"Where?"

"The bike racks," she said. "My brother's waiting. He's impatient."

I thought of Sam, probably vibrating near the gate, imagining my mysterious disappearance.

"Okay," I said. "But my brother's waiting too."

She grinned. "You have a brother?"

"You'll meet him," I said grimly. "You won't miss him."

We walked side by side toward the bike racks.

The late afternoon sun stretched shadows across the concrete. My schoolbag thumped against my hip, but I didn't care.

"So," I said. "Tell me about the note."

She nodded. Reached into her pocket.

"This showed up on my desk yesterday," she said.

She unfolded the paper and handed it to me.

It wasn't pink.

It was yellow.

And the handwriting was nothing like hers.

It was messy. Slanted. Pressed hard into the paper, as if the person writing wanted to make sure it stayed forever.

I know what you did.

That was all it said.

My mouth went dry.

"That's not great," I said carefully.

"No," she agreed. "It's not."

"What did you do?" I asked, then immediately regretted how that sounded. "I mean—you don't have to tell me."

She stopped walking.

"I did nothing wrong," she said. "Not really."

That wasn't comforting.

"I just—" she sighed. "I moved something I shouldn't have."

"What kind of something?"

Her brother's voice cut across the yard before she could answer.

"MIA! You said TWO MINUTES!"

A boy about Sam's age stood by the bike racks, helmet on, hopping from foot to foot. He looked like he'd had too much sugar and not enough patience.

"That's Toby," she said. "Ignore him."

Too late.

Sam came running toward us at full speed, skidding to a stop beside me.

"LEO," he whispered loudly. "YOU WERE GONE FOR AGES."

"This is Mia," I said. "And Toby."

Sam stared at Toby's helmet. "Is that a meteor design?"

Toby's face lit up. "It's actually the Perseid shower."

Sam gasped. "NO WAY."

They were instantly friends.

Mia looked at me. "Your brother's energetic."

"That's one word for it," I said.

She took a breath. "Can you help me?"

I looked down at the yellow note again.

"I think I already am," I said.

And somehow, without meaning to, I knew this wasn't just about a piece of paper anymore.

It was about secrets.

And once you noticed them, you couldn't unsee them.

CHAPTER 3

Things That Do Not Stay Put

That night, I couldn't sleep. This wasn't unusual dramatically—I wasn't a kid who stared at the ceiling every night thinking deep thoughts—but this was different. This was when your brain refused to stop talking, even when you told it politely to shut up.

I know what you did.

Those words kept rearranging themselves in my head like fridge magnets.

I know what you did.

You did something. I know something.

I turned onto my side, then onto my other side, then onto my back. The glow-in-the-dark stars on my ceiling, Sam's old ones, because he'd upgraded to "realistic constellations," floated quietly above me, smug and unhelpful.

From the other bed, Sam sighed in his sleep and muttered, "Saturn... rings..."

Of course, he did. I sat up. If I were being honest, and I usually was, even when it was inconvenient, I knew two things for certain: one, Mia Collins was scared, and two: whatever she'd "moved" wasn't supposed to be found.

And somehow, impossibly, I was now involved.

At breakfast, Mum slid a bowl of cereal in front of me.

"You're quiet," she said.

"I'm thinking," I replied.

"That's worrying," Dad said without looking up from his phone.

Sam spooned cereal into his mouth at top speed. "Leo's involved in a mystery," he announced, spraying milk.

I kicked him under the table.

"Ow," he said, pleased. "See? Mystery confirmed."

I grabbed my bag and stood up. "We're going to be late."

Mum and Dad looked at each other but said nothing.

At school, everything looked the same, which annoyed me.

The lockers were still dented. The corridor still smelled of fake lemon. Kids still laughed too loudly or not at all. But I wasn't the same, and that felt unfair.

Once you knew something important, the world was supposed to react.

Flicker or change colour, maybe even play dramatic music.

It didn't.

I spotted Mia near the drinking taps before class.

She was pretending to listen to a girl with glittery hair clips, but her eyes flicked up the second she saw me.

At lunch, she found me behind the library, where the concrete wall had a crack shaped like Australia.

"Did you think about it?" she asked.

"Yes," I said. "A lot."

"Good," she said. "Because I need to show you something."

That was becoming a pattern.

She led me to the art room, which was empty.

She knelt and reached under the sink, pulling out a shoebox.

My stomach tightened.

"This is where it was," she said. "Before."

"Where *what* was?"

She opened the lid.

Inside were folded papers, lots of them.

Different colours. Pink, yellow, blue, some white.

All creased, and all written on.

Notes.

I stared.

"How many are there?" I whispered.

"Twenty-three," she said. "I counted."

That was too many notes. Notes were supposed to be one or two. Twenty-three meant effort, planning and time, lots of time.

"Where did you get these?" I asked.

"They weren't mine," she blurted.

"I swear. I found them. In the caretaker's cupboard. Behind the sports mats."

I frowned. "Why were you in there?"

She hesitated.

"I dropped my sketchbook," she said.

"It slid under the door. I went to get it, and they were just there." She shrugged helplessly.

"And you moved them," I said.

She nodded. "I panicked. I didn't know what to do. I thought if someone else found them..."

"They might get in trouble," I finished.

"Yes," she said. "Or worse."

I picked one note at random.

Stop watching.

Another: *You shouldn't be here.*

Another: *This isn't your story.*

A chilly feeling crept up my spine.

"These aren't jokes," I said.

"No," she agreed. "And now someone knows I touched them."

"Or thinks you did something else," I said.

She looked at me. "What if they think I wrote them?"

That thought settled heavily between us.

"Who would write notes like this?" I asked.

She shook her head. "That's why I needed you."

I swallowed. "Because I look."

"Yes."

I looked around the room, at the door, at the window, and at the shadows. Nothing obvious, which was the problem.

"First rule," I said, surprising myself, "nothing stays hidden forever."

She blinked. "Is that a rule?"

"It is now," I said as I stuffed the notes in my pocket.

After school, Sam cornered me near the gate.

"So," he said. "Mia mystery update?"

"You are not involved," I said.

"That's what you said last time," he replied smugly. "And then Toby told me someone's writing secret notes, and that's basically espionage."

I groaned.

"Fine," I said. "But you don't tell anyone."

"Not even Mum?"

"Especially not Mum."

That night, I spread the notes out on my bedroom floor.

Sam lay beside me, propped on his elbows.

"They're like signals," he said.

"What signals?"

"Like in space," he said. "When someone sends a message but doesn't want to be found."

I paused, looked at Sam, and said: "That's actually not terrible thinking."

Sam beamed.

I studied the handwriting. The pressure. The slant.

"The same person wrote these," I said.

"How do you know?"

"They push down hard on certain letters," I said. "Like they're angry. Or scared."

Sam pointed. "That one's different."

He was right. One note, white paper, smaller than the rest, had softer writing.

Be careful.

I stared at it.

"That one doesn't belong," I said.

"Maybe it's a warning," Sam said.

"Or someone else interfering," I said.

Sam's eyes widened. "Multiple operatives."

"Go to sleep," I said automatically.

But I couldn't stop thinking.

The next day, Mia didn't come to school.

By lunchtime, I was officially worried.

By the last bell, I was officially terrified.

Sam jogged beside me. "She'll be okay."

"You don't know that."

"I know people don't disappear that easily," he said. "Unless there's a black hole."

That night, my pocket buzzed, and I pulled out my phone. A message from an unknown number.

Stop looking.

I stared at the screen, my heart pounding.

Somewhere down the hall, Sam was humming the theme from a space documentary.

And for the first time, I understood something important. Notes weren't just messages.

They were doors, and once you opened one, you couldn't pretend you didn't see what was on the other side.

CHAPTER 4

The Rules of Being Watched

The message stayed on my screen for exactly three seconds before I locked my phone and shoved it under my pillow as if it might explode.

Stop looking.

That wasn't a joke. Jokes had punchlines. That was a command.

I lay still, listening to the house breathe around me. The tick of the hallway clock, the low hum of the fridge, Sam's door creaking as he rolled over in his sleep. Everything sounded normal, which somehow made it worse. Bad things weren't supposed to arrive quietly. They crashed in with sirens or thunder, or at least dramatic music.

This had arrived politely. Like it knew where I lived.

I slept little after that.

Every time my eyes closed, I pictured someone standing outside my window, watching glow-in-the-dark stars and two boys who were supposed to be ordinary.

In the morning, Mum noticed.

"You look like you wrestled a pillow and lost," she said, sliding toast onto my plate.

"I'm fine," I said automatically.

Sam leaned over, cereal spoon paused mid-air. "He's lying."

"Sam," Mum warned.

"He was awake," Sam continued, unfazed. "I heard him whispering."

"I was not whispering," I said.

"You said, 'stop looking,'" Sam replied.

The room went silent.

Mum frowned. "What were you watching, Leo?"

I swallowed. "A documentary."

Sam nodded enthusiastically. "About surveillance."

I kicked him again.

At school, Mia was back.

Relief hit me so fast it almost knocked me over. She stood near the lockers, backpack hugged tight to her chest, eyes scanning the corridor like it might bite.

She saw me and walked over quickly.

"I got a message," she whispered.

"So did I." Then I showed her my screen.

Her face drained of colour.

"Same words?" she asked.

"Yes."

We stood there, two kids pretending not to be scared in a hallway full of lockers and footsteps.

"They know," she said.

"They don't know everything," I replied. I wasn't sure why I believed that, but I did. "If they did, they wouldn't warn us. They'd just act."

She nodded slowly. "What do we do?"

I thought of the notes, the shoebox, and the white warning slip.

"We make the rules," I said.

"Rules?"

"Yes," I said. "For being watched."

She blinked. "That's unsettlingly confident."

"I'm nervous, and nervous people make plans." I admitted.

At recess, we sat behind the gym, backs to the wall.

"Rule one," I said. "We don't keep the notes in one place anymore."

"I already moved them," Mia said. "Split them. Different hiding spots."

"Good," I said. "Rule two: no messages on phones. Phones can be tracked."

She grimaced. "Then how do we talk?"

I hesitated. "We don't. Not unless we're together."

"That's inconvenient."

"Danger usually is."

She smiled faintly at that.

"Rule three," I continued. "We don't tell anyone else."

Sam's face popped into my mind immediately.

"...Mostly," I amended.

After school, Sam cornered me in my room.

"You're terrible at keeping secrets," he said.

"I am excellent at keeping secrets."

"No, you are not. You're thinking loudly."

I sighed. "Someone told me to stop looking."

Sam's eyes lit up. Not with fear, but with excitement.

"Threatening contact. Classic escalation."

"This isn't a game, Sam."

"I know," he said seriously. "That's why it's interesting."

I sat on the bed. "We need to figure out who's writing the notes."

Sam climbed up beside me. "Okay. Let's start with motive."

"You've been watching detective shows again."

"Yes," he said. "They're educational."

We made a list of people who liked control, of people who liked secrets, and of people who spent time alone.

"Teachers?" Sam suggested.

"Too obvious."

"The caretaker?"

I froze.

The caretaker. Mr Bell. Quiet. Always around. Always watching. The cupboard. The mats.

My stomach twisted.

"Maybe," I said carefully.

The next day, Mia and I watched Mr Bell from the oval. He swept leaves slowly and methodically.

"Does he look suspicious?" she whispered.

"He looks... thorough," I said. "Which is worse?"

That afternoon, I found another note.

This one was blue. Tucked into my locker.

You broke a rule.

My hands shook.

I didn't tell Mia straight away. I didn't tell Sam. I went to the bathroom and stared at my reflection, trying to look brave.

I am not brave. I am nine and scared and suddenly very aware of how small I am.

At home, Sam noticed anyway.

"You're pale," he said. "Like astronauts before launch."

I showed him the note, and he read it carefully.

"They're bluffing," he said.

"How do you know?"

"Because they didn't say which rule."

That stopped me.

"You're right," I drawled.

"They want you to panic, and when you panic, you make mistakes."

I stared at my little brother. "When did you get smart?"

"I've always been smart," he said. "I'm just shorter."

That night, Mia slipped a folded piece of paper into my hand as we left school.

White.

Tomorrow. Library. 3:30.

No signature. But I knew.

At 3:30, the library was nearly empty. Dust motes floated like tiny planets.

Mia was already there. So was someone else.

A girl from Year Five. Tall. Confident. Glitter clips.

"I'm glad you came," she said.

My heart hammered.

"Who are you?" I asked.

She smiled. "Someone who's tired of watching."

And suddenly I understood something else.

One person did not write the notes.

They had never been, and the scariest secrets weren't about what you'd done; they were about who else knew.

As the librarian coughed loudly at the desk, I realised Tuesday hadn't just stopped being invisible.

It had turned into something else entirely.

A beginning.

CHAPTER 5

The Ones Who See

The girl from Year Five didn't sit down straight away. She stood there with her arms folded, leaning against one of the tall shelves as if this was her library and we'd just wandered into it by mistake.

Up close, I could see her glittery hair clips weren't random—they were shaped like stars. Not the cute kind. The sharp, pointy kind.

"You're Leo," she said.

I didn't like the way she said my name.

"And you're Mia," she added, turning slightly. "You're harder to pin down."

Mia stiffened beside me.

"Who are you?" Mia asked again, firmer this time.

The girl sighed as if we were being slow on purpose.

"Zara Finch," she said. "Year Five. And before you ask—no, I'm not the one writing the notes. I'm the one who found out about them."

"That's not comforting," I said.

She smiled at me then, quick, and sharp. "It shouldn't be."

We sat, and the chairs scraped softly against the carpet, loud enough that the librarian glanced up, eyes narrowing before returning to her computer.

Zara leaned forward.

"There are three kinds of people in this school," she said. "The ones who watch, the ones who are watched, and the ones who pretend nothing's happening, and you, Leo, you are a watcher."

Mia glanced at me, surprised.

"And you," Zara continued, nodding at Mia, "are someone who accidentally stepped into the wrong space."

Mia bristled. "I did nothing wrong."

"I know," Zara said. "That's how it always starts."

I folded my hands in my lap, partly to stop them from shaking.

"Why are you telling us this?" I asked.

"Because the notes are escalating," Zara said. "And because whoever's behind them doesn't like competition."

"Competition for what?" Mia asked.

"For information," Zara replied.

"You said you're tired of watching," I said. "So why not just... tell a teacher?"

Zara laughed. Actually laughed.

"You think teachers don't know?" she said. "They always know *something*. They just don't know what to do with it. Or they decide it's easier not to."

My chest tightened. I hated how reasonable she sounded.

"There's a group," she went on. "Not official. Just kids. From different years. We notice patterns. Things that don't add up."

My heart skipped. "How many?"

"Enough," she said. "And fewer every year."

"Why fewer?" Mia asked quietly.

Zara didn't answer straight away.

"Because people get scared," she said finally. "Or warned. Or blamed."

The image of the yellow note flashed in my head.

I know what you did.

"What do you want from us?" I asked.

Zara tilted her head. "I want to know what you found."

Mia and I exchanged a look.

"No," Mia said quickly. "That's not—"

"Twenty-three notes," Zara interrupted calmly. "Different colours. Same pressure patterns. One white outlier."

Mia's mouth opened, and my stomach dropped.

"You've been watching *us*," I said.

"Yes," Zara said. "Because once you move the notes, you become part of the system."

"That's not fair," Mia said, her voice shaking now.

"No," Zara agreed. "It isn't."

The librarian coughed again, louder this time.

Zara leaned back. "Relax. I'm not your enemy."

"That's what enemies say," I muttered.

She smirked. "True."

We left the library separately. Zara first, then Mia, and then me, after a full minute of pretending to read a book about famous bridges.

Outside, Sam was waiting by the fence, swinging his backpack like a wrecking ball.

"YOU WERE IN THERE FOREVER," he stage-whispered. "Did you meet her?"

"Her?" I asked.

"The tall one," he said. "With the stars. Toby says she runs things."

My blood went cold.

"Runs what?"

Sam shrugged. "Stuff. Also, she borrowed his pencil once and never gave it back."

That night, I lay awake again.

But this time, it wasn't fear keeping me up.

It was anger.

Someone had decided we were pieces on a board we didn't even know existed. Someone thought notes and warnings were enough to control people.

I didn't like that.

The next day, I broke Rule Two.

I wrote a note.

Not on pink, or yellow, or blue, but on plain white paper.

I see you too.

I folded it once. Carefully. Deliberately.

And I slipped it into locker 219.

Not mine.

Not Mia's.

Mr Bell's locker.

Because if there was one thing I knew now, it was this:

Watching only worked if you stayed invisible.

And I was done with invisible.

CHAPTER 6

How to Declare War

The thing about writing a note that says *I see you too* is that it feels extremely powerful for about twelve seconds.

After that, it feels like you've just poked a sleeping bear with a stick and realised the stick is actually a noodle.

I discovered this feeling at approximately 9:07 a.m. the next morning, while standing in line for assembly, when my stomach began doing complicated gymnastics it had not trained for.

Sam noticed immediately.

"You look like you swallowed the moon," he said.

"That's not a thing," I replied.

"It is if you're nervous," he said. "Your face goes all, well, crater-y."

"I am not nervous."

"You wrote a note, didn't you?" he whispered.

"You don't know that."

"You get this look," Sam said. "Like when you tried to microwave a fork."

"That was one time."

"And it exploded."

"Quiet," I hissed.

Assembly droned on. Something about responsibility, something about hats. I tried not to imagine Mr Bell opening his locker and finding my note sitting there like a smug little rectangle of doom.

I tried not to imagine him knowing it was me, and I failed at both.

By recess, nothing had happened which was worse.

Mia found me near the bubblers, fiddling with the tap like it might reveal answers if I turned it just right.

"Are you okay?" she asked.

"I may have done something bold," I said.

She narrowed her eyes. "Define bold."

"I wrote a note back."

Her eyes widened. "Leo."

"I know."

"You broke Rule One AND Rule Two."

"I also used white paper," I added. "So, technically—"

"Leo."

"I slipped it into Mr Bell's locker."

She stared at me, and then she laughed.

Not a polite laugh, but a full, surprised, slightly hysterical laugh that made two Year Twos stop and stare.

"You're insane," she said.

"I prefer proactive," I replied.

She wiped her eyes. "Do you realise what you've done?"

"Yes," I said. "I've probably shortened my lifespan."

"But also," she said slowly, "you've changed the rules."

That sounded better.

Sam jogged over, skidding to a stop.

"Is this about the note?" he asked brightly.

"Yes," we both said at once.

He grinned. "I knew it."

At lunch, things escalated.

I was halfway through my sandwich when a shadow fell across our table. I looked up.

Zara Finch.

She didn't sit down, and she didn't smile. She just looked at me like I was a math problem that had answered back.

"You wrote to him," she said.

I swallowed a bite of bread that suddenly felt like glue.

"You've been busy," I replied weakly.

"That was reckless," she said.

"Maybe," I said. "But it was also educational."

She raised an eyebrow. "Oh?"

"Yes," I said. "Because now I know you're not the only one watching."

Her lips twitched. "You figured that out already."

"And I know the notes aren't just about fear," I continued. "They're about control. And control doesn't like surprises."

Sam leaned across the table. "He's been practising speeches."

"I have not."

"A little," Mia whispered.

Zara studied me for a long moment.

"You realise," she said finally, "that once you challenge the system, it responds."

"I'm counting on it," I said.

She exhaled slowly.

"You are either very brave or very stupid."

"Can't I be both?"

She snorted despite herself.

That afternoon, the response arrived, not in a note but in an announcement.

"Leo Marshall, please come to the front office."

Every head in the classroom turned.

Mrs Calder gave me *the look*.

My legs felt like cooked spaghetti, but I stood.

Sam caught my eye as I passed by his classroom and gave me a thumbs-up, then mouthed, *If you're arrested, I want your Lego.*

The front office smelled of carpet and mild panic Mr Bell stood near the counter and he was smiling.

This was not comforting.

"Leo," he said warmly. "Have a seat."

I sat.

"So," he continued, "you like notes."

I stared at him.

"I don't know what you mean."

He chuckled. "Straight to denial. Admirable."

My heart thudded.

"I found something in my locker," he said. "Very thoughtful."

I waited.

"You have good handwriting," he added.

"That's not true," I blurted. "My teacher says it looks like frightened ants."

He laughed. Actually laughed.

"That's funny," he said. "You know what else is funny?"

I shook my head.

"How observant you are."

There it was.

"I don't understand," I said, because sometimes pretending is useful.

Mr Bell leaned closer.

"People think watching is about power," he said. "It's not. It's about order."

I nodded slowly, as if I were considering it, while mentally screaming.

"But order," he continued, "only works when everyone agrees to it."

"And what if they don't?" I asked.

His smile thinned.

"Then things get messy."

I stood. "Am I in trouble?"

He straightened. "Not today."

That felt worse than yes.

Back in class, Mia was waiting, eyes wide.

"He talked to you," she whispered.

"Yes."

"And?"

"I think," I said, "we've officially annoyed him."

The bell rang, and we got up to go to our next class when Sam bounced up beside us. "What happened? Did he monologue? Villains always monologue."

"He didn't twirl a moustache," I said. "But it was close."

That evening at home after dinner, I sat at my desk, staring at a blank piece of paper.

"Don't," Sam warned from his bed.

"I have to," I said.

"You're going to start a paper war."

"Already did."

I wrote carefully. Not to Mr Bell. Not to Zara.

To whomever had written the white warning note.

Thanks for the heads-up. Want to talk?

Sam leaned over. "You're networking with mysterious informants now."

"Yes," I said. "It's very grown-up."

I slipped the note into my bag.

Because if there was one thing I'd learned, it was this: once you see the hidden things, you can't stop.

And honestly?

For the first time in my life, that felt kind of awesome.

CHAPTER 7

Councils, Constellations, and Other Dangerous Things

Leo + Mia + Zara

Zara picked the meeting place, of course. Not because she said, *Meet me here,* like she was some kind of movie boss, but because she simply appeared in the place that made the most sense for someone who liked control.

The far corner of the oval.

Behind the storage shed, where the grass was a bit dead and the wind always seemed to be annoyed.

Mia and I arrived together, walking as if we were casual, which is hard to do when you feel like your spine is made of alarm bells.

Zara was already there, sitting cross-legged on the concrete step, a folder on her lap.

A *folder*.

Nobody in our age group carried folders unless they were (a) trying to impress a teacher, or (b) organising a rebellion.

She didn't look up straight away.

"That took you long enough," she said.

"We came at exactly the time you texted," Mia replied.

Zara finally lifted her eyes. "And yet, in my mind, you were still late."

I sat down anyway, because sometimes you don't have the energy to argue with Year Fives, who radiate authority like heat.

"So," Zara said, tapping the folder. "You poked the bear."

"I wrote a note," I corrected. "A small one."

"And then got called to the front office," she replied. "Which means he noticed."

"I wanted him to," I said.

Zara stared at me like I'd just announced I wanted to juggle chainsaws for fun.

"Leo," Mia said softly, "maybe we should..."

"No," I cut in, then regretted how sharp it sounded. I took a breath. "Look, Mr Bell has been doing this for a long time. So long, for I don't even know how long. See notes; fear. People shutting up. If we keep whispering, we stay trapped."

Zara's mouth twitched. "You have a point. Unfortunately."

"I'm not trying to be reckless," I said. "I'm trying to make him slip."

"How do you make someone like that slip?" Mia asked.

Zara opened the folder.

Inside were pages, not notes but copies. Handwritten re-writes, dates, little arrows, and circles. A map of the school drawn from memory and a list of names.

My throat went dry.

"You've been doing homework," I said.

"I've been doing *survival*," Zara replied. "There's a differ-ence."

She slid the folder between us and pointed.

"These are the places notes have shown up," she said. "Lockers. Desk trays. Sports bags. A library book. Once—" she paused, face tightening "—inside a kid's lunchbox."

"That's creepy," Mia whispered.

"It's worse than creepy," Zara said. "It's intentional. It says, *I can reach into your normal life whenever I want.*"

I stared at the map. "What's the pattern?"

Zara's eyes flicked to me. "That's what I wanted you to tell me."

"What?"

"You're the watcher," she said. "You notice things other people miss. Tell me—what do you see?"

I hated that my stomach warmed a little, and I also hated that I enjoyed being useful, so I leaned in and studied the marked spots.

The lockers were clustered near the main corridor. The desk trays were in rooms close to the office.

The sports bags were in the equipment shed. The lunchbox that could have been anywhere.

I looked closely and then drew a line with my finger.

"Look, these locations have something in common." I remarked.

"Yes, you are right. I see that now. Okay, go on," Zara said.

"They're all places where adults can move without being questioned," I said slowly. "Mr Bell, teachers, duty staff. Anyone in a high-vis vest."

Mia frowned. "But kids can move around too."

"Yes," I said, "but kids get stopped. Adults don't."

Zara nodded, satisfied. "Good. What else?"

I stared again, then something prickled at the back of my mind like a splinter.

"There's something about timing," I said.

Zara raised an eyebrow. "Explain."

"Some notes are daytime notes," I said. "Bold ones. Like they want to be *felt* immediately. While some others are left after school. Quieter. Like warning notes."

Mia's eyes widened. "The white one."

"Yes," I said. "That one wasn't meant to scare. It was meant to help."

Zara's face tightened. "And that means—"

"Someone inside the system is leaking," I finished.

We all went silent.

Even the wind seemed to pause.

Mia hugged her knees. "But why?"

Zara stared at the grass as if it might answer. "Guilt, or anger, or possibly fear."

"Or they're being targeted too," I said.

Zara looked at me sharply.

"You think the warning note person is a victim?"

"Maybe," I said. "Or maybe they're trying to stop it."

Mia's voice went smaller.

"What if they're just trying to recruit us?"

Zara leaned back, rubbing her forehead like a stressed adult.

"Great," she muttered. "Now we have layers."

I tried to smile, but it came out crooked. "Mysteries usually do."

Zara shut the folder. "Okay. New plan."

Mia tensed. "I thought we had rules."

"We do," Zara said. "But we also need a strategy. Here's what we're doing: we're going to force another note."

"Force a note?" I repeated.

Zara nodded.

"A trap. Something harmless but irresistible. Something that looks like a secret."

Mia's face paled. "Like bait."

"Exactly," Zara said.

"We plant it somewhere he likes to work. Somewhere he thinks he owns."

"The caretaker's cupboard," Mia whispered.

Zara nodded. "And we watch who checks it."

My heart started thumping again.

"Who's 'we'?" I asked.

Zara looked at me as if I'd missed something obvious. "You. Me. Mia. And—" her gaze flicked over my shoulder.

I turned.

Sam and Toby were approaching, deep in conversation, not even pretending they weren't.

"Oh no," I groaned.

Mia blinked. "Are they okay?"

Sam was waving his hands as if he was guiding a plane in. Toby nodded solemnly, as if receiving sacred knowledge.

"They're fine," I said. "They're always like that."

Zara stared at them. "Why are they walking like generals?"

"Because in their heads," I said tiredly, "they're in a space war."

Zara exhaled. "This is going to get messy."

"Welcome to my life," I said.

And as Sam reached us, grinning like he'd discovered a new planet, I realised something else:

If Zara's plan works, we'd get answers.

And if it didn't...

Well. Then we'd find out what happened when you poked a bear twice.

Sam + Toby

Sam and Toby didn't think they were "eavesdropping."

They thought they were "conducting parallel intelligence operations."

Which is the thing you think when you're seven, obsessed with space, and slightly convinced your older brother is secretly the main character in a spy movie.

They walked side-by-side across the oval, their backpacks bumping in rhythm like they'd practised. Sam's galaxy hoodie was zipped all the way up even though it wasn't that cold because Sam believed you couldn't discuss serious things without appropriate clothing.

Toby, still wearing his Perseid helmet (yes, even on foot, because Toby was committed), leaned in.

"So, the notes," Toby whispered. "You think they're like signals."

Sam nodded intensely. "Definitely. Like when astronauts send messages back to Earth. Except these are evil."

Toby's eyes widened. "Evil space messages?"

"Not from space," Sam clarified. "From *inside the base*."

Toby gasped. "A traitor?"

"Maybe," Sam said. "Or a malfunctioning robot."

Toby looked thoughtful.

"Mr Bell walks like a robot."

Sam snapped his fingers.

"Exactly! And he's always near the maintenance stuff. Maintenance is where robots live."

Toby nodded, absorbing this with total seriousness. "Also, he sweeps in straight lines."

"Robots love straight lines," Sam said.

They reached the edge of the storage shed and paused, watching Leo, Mia, and Zara in the distance.

"They look like they're planning," Toby whispered.

"They are," Sam said. "Leo is doing his planning face."

"What does that look like?"

"Like he's trying not to throw up, but also wants to look cool," Sam replied.

Toby blinked. "That's very specific."

Sam shrugged. "I know my brother."

Toby leaned closer.

"Do you think Leo will become famous?"

Sam nodded immediately. "Probably."

"For what?"

"Solving the note mystery," Sam said. "And saving the school. And maybe even Australia."

Toby looked impressed.

"Australia is big."

"It's okay," Sam assured him. "Leo is dramatic."

They sat in the grass near the shed like two tiny surveillance agents, whispering about their theories.

Toby pulled a crumpled piece of paper from his pocket. "I made a list."

Sam's eyes lit up. "You made a list?"

Toby nodded proudly. "Suspects."

Sam leaned in. "Okay. Who?"

Toby cleared his throat as if he were about to present a scientific report.

"One: Mr Bell," Toby said. "Because he's quiet and knows doors."

Sam nodded. "And robots."

"Two: Mrs Calder," Toby continued. "Because she has sharp eyebrows and sharp people write sharp notes."

Sam considered this. "Mrs Calder *could* write 'Stop looking' without blinking."

"Three," Toby said, lowering his voice, "the librarian."

Sam gasped. "Mrs Dalloway?"

Toby nodded gravely. "She knows all the secrets because books are secrets."

Sam's mind whirred. "But she's always saying, 'No running.' That's an excellent cover."

Toby's eyes shone. "Exactly."

Sam grabbed a stick and began drawing in the dirt.

"This is the school," he said, sketching a lopsided rectangle. "This is the office. This is the locker zone."

Toby watched, impressed. "You draw fast."

"I'm a tactical thinker," Sam said.

Toby pointed at the map. "Where would you hide notes?"

Sam tapped the dirt thoughtfully. "In places people don't look. Under things. Inside things. Like a sandwich."

Toby shuddered. "That lunchbox thing is terrifying."

Sam nodded. "It is psychological warfare."

Toby hesitated. "Do you think... they're watching us right now?"

Sam looked around dramatically, squinting into the air as if he could see invisible cameras.

"If they are," he said, "then they'll know we know."

Toby gulped. "Is that good?"

"It's brave," Sam decided. "Also, Leo said being invisible is bad now."

Toby nodded. "So, we should be visible."

Sam stood up suddenly and waved both arms wildly at the empty oval.

"WE SEE YOU!" he shouted.

Toby's eyes went huge. "SAM!"

Sam grinned. "Visibility!"

From across the oval, Leo snapped his head around with a look that could melt metal.

Sam sat back down quickly.

"Okay," he whispered, "maybe not *that* visible."

Toby leaned in again. "What's our job, then?"

Sam stared at the older kids plotting by the shed, then back at his dirt map.

"Our job," he said, "is to support the mission."

"How?" Toby asked.

Sam smiled with total confidence, like he had no idea how dangerous confidence could be.

"We collect data," Sam said. "We listen. We watch. We find patterns. And if anyone tries to scare Leo..."

He paused, eyes narrowing like a tiny astronaut preparing for launch.

"We become annoying," Sam finished.

Toby blinked. "Annoying?"

"The most powerful force in the universe," Sam said solemnly, "is a kid who won't stop asking questions."

Toby looked at him as if he'd just spoken the truth of the cosmos.

Then Toby nodded. "Okay. I can do annoying."

Sam grinned. "Good. Because I'm already excellent at it."

And as they marched toward the shed.

Two small, clumsy satellites orbiting a much bigger problem, and Sam felt something he didn't quite have a word for yet.

It wasn't fear; it was purpose.

Also, he still wanted Leo's Lego if Leo got arrested.

But he didn't say that part aloud.

CHAPTER 8

Bait, Betrayal, and the Discovery of Cooties

If someone had told me that the most dangerous part of our very serious plan to catch a secret note-writing menace would be *my face*, I would have laughed.

I would have laughed confidently, and I would have been wrong.

We met after school in the art room because Zara said it had "multiple exits and plausible excuses," which sounded like something you learned in spy school or from watching too many documentaries. She immediately took charge, spreading papers across the big table like she was dealing cards in a very intense game.

"Okay," Zara said. "Bait has to be believable, irresistible, and harmless."

"Like free cake," Sam said from the doorway.

"This is not about cake," Zara said without looking up.

"Everything is about cake," Sam replied, and Toby nodded as if this was scientific fact.

Mia sat beside me, close enough that I could smell her shampoo. She smelled like apples, or maybe pears, or something fruit-adjacent and distracting.

I shifted in my chair.

Focus, Leo. Notes. Menace. Bear-poking.

"Here's the idea," Zara said.

"We plant a note that *looks* like it reveals something valuable. A secret. Something someone watching wouldn't be able to ignore."

"Like what?" I asked.

Zara tapped her pen against her teeth. "Like a list."

"A list of what?" Mia asked.

"Names," Zara said. "Places. Times. Enough to make it look real."

My stomach tightened. "But not real."

"Obviously," Zara said. "We're not monsters."

Sam raised his hand. "What if it's a list of planets?"

Everyone stared at him.

"What?" he said. "Planets are precious."

"Sam," I said gently, "no one is threatening kids with space facts."

"Yet," he muttered.

Zara slid a blank sheet of yellow paper toward me.

"You write it."

"Me?" I squeaked.

"Yes," she said. "Your handwriting is messy but intentional. It looks authentic."

"That is the nicest insult anyone's ever given me," I said.

Mia smiled at me. My brain did a small, inconvenient flip.

I picked up the pen.

"What should it say?" I asked.

Zara leaned in. "Start with something that looks like a discovery. Something that suggests the watcher has been exposed."

I thought for a moment, then wrote carefully:

I know where you leave the notes.

My hand shook a little.

"Good," Zara said. "Now add a time."

"After school," I wrote.

"And a place," Mia whispered.

I hesitated. "The caretaker's cupboard?"

Zara nodded. "Perfect."

I added it and then stopped.

"This feels like lying," I said.

"It's strategic misdirection," Zara replied.

Sam leaned over my shoulder.

"That's lying with confidence."

I finished the note and folded it once. Cleanly.

Zara nodded. "We'll plant it together. Then we wait."

"Wait. Where?" I asked.

She smirked. "Not together."

Of course.

We split up.

Zara went to "create background noise," which apparently meant volunteering to help a teacher carry sports equipment. Sam and Toby were instructed to "be normal," which they interpreted creatively by walking laps around the oval pretending to be satellites.

Mia and I were left alone in the art room.

I suddenly became extremely aware of my hands again.

Mia was quiet. Not nervous-quiet. Thinking-quiet.

"You, okay?" I asked.

She nodded, then shook her head, then laughed softly. "Sorry. I'm just this is a lot."

"Yeah," I agreed. "My Tuesdays used to be beige."

She smiled. "Mine too."

We stood there, not moving. The note sat on the table between us, folded and waiting, as if it knew it was important.

"You know," Mia said, "when I first wrote you that pink note, I almost didn't."

"Why?" I asked.

"Because you looked busy," she said. "And because I didn't want to be wrong about you."

I frowned. "Wrong how?"

She met my eyes. "Wrong about you being kind."

Something warm spread through my chest again. Uncomfortable. Not unpleasant.

"I gave a kid an apple," I said. "That's not exactly heroic."

"It was to him," she said.

We stood there another second too long.

Then she leaned in.

It wasn't fast. It wasn't dramatic. It was careful, like she was checking if the ground was safe.

Her lips brushed my cheek.

Just barely.

My brain shut down completely.

There was a buzzing sound in my ears, like someone had turned on static. My face felt hot. My legs forgot their job.

"Sorry," she blurted. "I just…"

"No," I blurted. "I mean, yes, sorry is fine, no, I…"

Smooth, Leo. Very smooth.

She laughed; cheeks were pink. "You don't have to say anything."

I nodded. Because speaking was currently beyond me.

Behind the supply shelves, two small heads slowly rose.

Sam's eyes were enormous.

Toby's mouth was open like he'd just seen a comet crash into the sun.

They stared.

They stared *hard*.

Then, Sam slowly lowered himself back down.

Toby whispered, loud enough to echo, "Did they just…"

"Yes," Sam whispered back. "They did."

"That was a kiss," Toby said, horrified.

"A cheek kiss," Sam corrected. "Still counts."

Toby clutched his helmet.

"My sister kissed your brother."

Sam swallowed. "My brother kissed your sister."

"They're *liking* each other," Toby whispered.

Sam shuddered. "Eek."

They scooted farther behind the shelves, as if proximity might be contagious.

"This changes everything," Toby said.

"How?" Sam asked.

"Feelings complicate missions," Toby said solemnly. "I saw it in a movie."

Sam nodded. "Also, cooties."

"Definitely cooties," Toby agreed.

Back at the table, Mia and I both pretended very hard that nothing had happened.

Which made everything worse.

"Okay, we should, uh, plant the bait." I said.

"Yes," Mia said, also too loudly. "The bait. Important bait."

We grabbed the note and headed toward the caretaker's cupboard, our shoulders bumping accidentally on purpose.

My cheek still tingled.

At the cupboard, Zara appeared as if she'd been waiting in the walls.

"Ready?" she asked.

"Yes," I said.

Mia slipped the note behind a stack of old sports cones, exactly where someone tidying would find it.

"Now," Zara said, "we wait."

The waiting was the worst. Minutes stretched. Shadows shifted. Every footstep made my heart jump.

Sam and Toby sat nearby, whispering furiously.

"I can't believe it," Sam said. "Leo is kissing adjacent."

"That's how it starts," Toby replied. "First cheeks. Then mouths."

Sam gagged. "Disgusting."

"They're siblings now," Toby said.

"No, they're not."

"They will be," Toby insisted. "That's how liking works."

Sam looked panicked. "Do I have to share Lego?"

"We need to monitor them," Toby said.

"For safety," Sam agreed.

An hour later, Mr Bell entered the cupboard. Zara tensed. I held my breath. He paused. Looked down.

Picked up the note. My heart hammered. He read it.

Then he smiled. Not a friendly smile. A tight one.

He folded the note and slipped it into his pocket.

Then he left.

Zara exhaled. "We've got him."

"Do we?" I asked.

"Yes," she said. "He took the bait."

Mia squeezed my hand without thinking. I didn't let go.

Sam watched this from across the room, eyes narrowing.

"They're holding hands now," he whispered.

Toby groaned. "It's spreading."

As we walked home, Mia stayed close to me. Not touching but aligned. Like we were on the same frequency.

"I didn't mean to surprise you," she said quietly.

"It was a delightful surprise," I admitted.

She smiled. "Good."

Behind us, Sam and Toby lagged, deep in discussion.

"We need a plan," Sam said.

"A counterplan," Toby agreed.

"For the notes?" Sam asked.

"No," Toby said gravely. "For the kissing."

Sam nodded. "Operation No More Eek."

I didn't hear the rest.

Because for the first time since all this started, I wasn't thinking about notes.

I was thinking about how sometimes, even in the middle of something scary and complicated, something warm sneaks in.

And maybe, just maybe, that was another kind of bait.

One the watcher wouldn't see coming at all.

CHAPTER 9

Scientific Evidence According to Dad

Dinner ended the way dinner always ended in our house: with Mum stacking plates like she was competing in a speed challenge, Dad rinsing things almost properly, and Sam announcing facts no one had asked for.

"Did you know," Sam said, pointing his fork at no one in particular, "that octopuses have three hearts?"

"Yes," Mum said. "And if you keep flicking peas, you'll see all three of mine give out."

Sam stopped flicking peas, technically.

I pushed my chair back and stood up.

"Study time," Mum said automatically.

Sam groaned as if she'd announced exile. "We were just learning."

"You were throwing food," Mum replied.

"Educational throwing," Sam muttered.

We went to our room, which we shared because apparently "character-building" meant learning how to ignore your brother breathing. Sam flopped onto his bed with a book about black holes. I sat at my desk, opened my maths workbook, and stared at the page as if it had offended me.

Fractions swam before my eyes.

My cheek still felt warm.

Which was ridiculous because cheeks were cheeks and they didn't keep memories.

Except mine, apparently, did.

I tapped my pencil.

Thought about the bait, Mr Bell, Zara's face when she'd said *we've got him,* Sam and Toby's horror and Mia's smile, and, of course, the kiss.

Okay, it was barely a kiss.

It was more like a friendly face acknowledgement.

But still.

My brain had decided it was important, very important, possibly *emergency important.*

I cleared my throat.

Sam didn't look up. "If you're about to say something weird, I want a warning."

"I'm going to ask Dad something," I said.

Sam's head snapped up. "Is it about the notes?"

"No."

"Is it about Mum?"

"No."

"Is it about—" Sam squinted. "—kissing?"

I stood up too fast.

"Why would it be about kissing?"

Sam's eyes widened slowly. "It *is* about kissing."

"No, it isn't."

"It is," he said smugly. "You're doing the face."

"What face?"

"The one where you look like you're thinking but also dying."

I grabbed my hoodie. "I'll be back."

"Where are you going?" Sam asked.

I didn't answer, and that made him sit up straighter.

"That's suspicious."

I left before he could ask more questions.

The kitchen was warm and loud with running water and clinking dishes. Mum was wiping the bench. Dad was stacking the dishwasher incorrectly, which Mum was pretending not to notice for the sake of peace.

I hovered for a second, suddenly very aware that this was not a normal thing to ask your parents.

But also, they were parents.

They'd done this before. Presumably without dying.

"Dad," I said.

He turned, smiling. "Yeah, mate?"

"Can I ask you a question?"

Mum froze mid-wipe.

Dad nodded. "Of course. What is it, Leo?"

I took a breath.

"How did you know you liked Mum when you kissed her for the first time?"

Silence, well, not quiet silence but an enormous silence.

The kind where the air goes still and even the dishwasher seems to pause out of respect.

Mum slowly turned around, and Dad blinked once, then twice.

Then he coughed.

"Well," he said. "That's a question."

Mum crossed her arms, lips twitching.

"I'm very interested in this answer."

Dad glanced at her. "You would be."

He looked back at me. "Why are you asking?"

I panicked.

"Science," I blurted.

Mum snorted.

Dad rubbed the back of his neck. "Okay. Science. Right."

He leaned against the counter as if he needed support.

"Well," he began, "first, it wasn't exactly like the movies."

"Did violins play?" I asked.

"No," Dad said. "There was traffic."

Mum laughed. "And a kebab shop."

Dad nodded. "Strong garlic presence."

This was not helping my mental image.

Dad continued, "I remember it clearly."

Mum raised an eyebrow. "Oh, do you now?"

"I do," Dad said, defensive. "I remember thinking, before it happened, that I was completely calm."

"Liar," Mum said.

"Okay, relatively calm," Dad corrected. "And then when it happened, I wasn't calm anymore."

"How?" I asked.

Dad thought for a moment.

"It was like my brain went quiet. Not empty. Just focused. Like everything else stopped competing for attention."

Mum softened. "That's actually not bad."

Dad brightened. "Thank you."

"So," I said slowly, "you knew because your brain was quiet?"

"Partly," Dad said. "But mostly because afterward, I wanted to stay."

"Stay?" I echoed.

"Yes," he said. "Not because I had to. Not because it was exciting. Just because being there felt right. Like I'd lined up with myself."

Mum rolled her eyes. "He practised that line later."

"It was true!" Dad protested.

Mum smiled at me.

"He also walked into a pole right after."

I blinked. "You did?"

Dad sighed. "I was distracted."

"That tracks," Mum said.

I considered this.

"So," I said, "if you don't know...?"

"Then that's okay too," Dad said quickly.

"Sometimes you don't know right away. Sometimes it takes time. Or more than one moment."

Mum nodded. "Or sometimes it's just a delightful moment. And that's allowed."

Dad glanced at her. "That's a good point."

"Of course it is," Mum said.

I shifted my weight. "What if you feel warm?"

Dad smiled. "Warmth is a good sign."

"What if your face does something weird?" I asked.

Mum laughed. "That is also normal."

"What if your brother sees it and looks traumatised?"

Dad snorted. "Very normal."

Mum leaned against the bench.

"The important thing, Leo, is this: liking someone isn't about fireworks or panic or thinking you're suddenly a different person."

Dad nodded. "It's about paying attention. About wanting the other person to be okay. About being a little braver than usual."

I swallowed.

"And about respecting them and yourself." Mum added.

Dad smiled at her. "She's better at this part."

"I know," Mum said.

I stood there, letting it all settle.

"So," Dad said gently, "did that help your... science?"

"Yes," I said honestly.

Mum tilted her head. "Do we need to know anything else?"

"No," I said quickly. "Definitely no."

Dad chuckled. "Alright, then."

I turned to leave, then hesitated.

"Dad?"

"Yes?"

"Did you ever panic after?"

Dad laughed. "Oh yes. Terribly."

Mum grinned. "He called his friend and asked if his heart was supposed to do that."

Dad shrugged. "It was a fair question."

I smiled.

Back in the room, Sam was waiting.

"So?" he demanded. "Did you ask?"

"Yes."

"And?"

I sat on my bed. "Dad walked into a pole."

Sam stared. "That explains a lot."

I lay back, staring at the ceiling stars.

For the first time all day, my brain was quiet.

Not empty.

Just lined up.

And that, apparently, was science.

CHAPTER 10

Saturday Plans and the Problem with Witnesses

Saturday mornings are supposed to feel different. They're meant to smell like toast and freedom. Like cartoons, you don't have to rush through and socks you don't have to find in a panic. Saturdays are the days when nothing important happens. Which is probably why something important always does.

I woke up early, before Sam, which almost never happened unless it was Christmas or I was about to be sick. The house was quiet in that soft way that makes everything feel bigger than it really is. Sunlight crept through the curtains, landing on my desk, my chair, the corner where my school bag sat as if it were pretending it wasn't full of secrets.

Yesterday kept replaying in my head.

The bait, Mr Bell's smile, Mia's hand squeezing mine, Sam's horrified whisper of *"It's spreading."*

I rolled onto my back and stared at the ceiling.

Today we had a meeting.

Not an official meeting; no one had sent an invitation or written minutes, but a meeting all the same.

Zara had called it "necessary recalibration," which was a worrying phrase for someone who still had a spelling list due on Monday.

By the time Sam woke up, I was already dressed and sitting at my desk, pretending to organise my books.

"You're awake early," Sam said suspiciously.

"I have plans."

"Plans-plans or secret-plans?"

I didn't answer.

Sam nodded. "Secret-plans."

After breakfast (during which Sam informed Mum that "romantic situations cause distraction and doom," which Mum ignored completely), we left for the park. The one near the old rotunda, where the grass was patchy and the swings always squeaked as if they were complaining.

Zara was already there.

She stood near the picnic table with a notebook under her arm, posture straight, expression serious, like the mayor of children.

Mia arrived a moment later, walking quickly, hair tied back, cheeks slightly pink. When she saw me, she smiled.

That smile did something to my insides that felt a lot like falling down one step you didn't know was there.

"Hi," she said.

"Hi," I said, which was apparently my word forever now.

Sam and Toby raced ahead of us, arguing loudly about whether black holes could technically eat secrets.

"They can," Sam insisted.

"Only if the secrets are matter," Toby replied.

"Secrets are emotional matter," Sam said confidently.

Zara cleared her throat.

"Okay, before the science team destabilises reality, we need to talk," she said.

We sat around the picnic table, and Zara stood.

"Update," she said. "Since the bait, there have been no new notes."

"That's good, right?" Mia asked.

"Or bad," Zara replied. "It means one of two things."

I sighed. "He's either cautious now..."

"...or planning," Zara finished.

Sam raised his hand. "Villains always plan."

Zara nodded. "Correct. Which is why we need to move next."

"Move how?" I asked.

Zara opened her notebook.

"We narrowed it down," she said. "We stop reacting and start controlling the environment."

"That sounds like something Mr Bell would say," I muttered.

"Yes," Zara said calmly. "And that's why it will work."

She pointed to the list that she had created.

"Next step: observation without provocation."

Sam frowned. "That sounds boring."

"It's not," Zara said. "It's patient."

Mia leaned toward me. "She means we watch without poking."

I nodded. "I can do that."

Zara continued. "We split into pairs. Cover different zones. No notes. No bait. Just patterns."

Sam pumped his fist. "Data collection!"

"Not you," Zara said immediately.

Sam deflated. "That's discrimination."

"You and Toby," Zara said, "are auxiliary observers."

Toby straightened proudly. "Auxiliary!"

Sam brightened. "That sounds important."

"It's very important," Zara said. "But it also means staying obvious. No sneaking."

Sam frowned. "I am physically incapable of subtlety."

"Perfect," Zara replied.

While Zara assigned zones, Mia shifted closer to me. Her hand brushed mine, just brushed.

My brain noticed immediately, too immediately, and then her fingers curled around mine.

It wasn't sudden; it wasn't dramatic.

It was gentle, like she was testing the idea before committing to it.

I didn't pull away.

My hand felt warm and steady, as if it belonged there.

I liked it a lot.

Something in my chest loosened, like a knot I hadn't realised was there.

I smiled without thinking, and then I felt it: that prickly awareness.

The *being seen,* feeling, and I looked up.

Toby was staring at us.

Not a quick glance, not curiosity.

Full, locked, and frozen.

His eyes moved from our hands to my face, to Mia's, and back to our hands.

His mouth opened slightly.

"Oh no," I whispered.

Mia followed my gaze and stiffened.

Toby turned slowly to Sam.

"They're holding hands," he said in a voice usually reserved for natural disasters.

Sam squinted. "No, they're not."

Toby pointed. "That."

Sam followed the finger.

He gasped.

"A SECOND TIME?" Sam whispered fiercely. "Already?"

"It's escalating," Toby said. "Rapidly."

Mia let go immediately, as if our hands had suddenly become dangerous animals.

My hand felt empty.

Zara looked up. "What?"

"Nothing," Sam said too quickly.

Toby nodded. "Nothing important."

Zara narrowed her eyes. "That usually means something extremely important."

"It's just," Sam struggled for words, "emotional developments."

Zara stared at me, then Mia, then exhaled. "I don't have time for this."

Mia's cheeks went red. "Sorry."

Zara waved it off.

"I don't care who likes whom. Just don't let it make you careless."

I nodded. "It won't."

Which was mostly true. Probably.

We broke up into groups.

Zara took the perimeter of the park and the nearby paths. Sam and Toby were assigned *"maximum visibility,"* which meant sitting near the playground loudly discussing suspects.

Mia and I were supposed to walk the path near the creek and "notice who noticed us."

We walked slowly, side by side, not touching this time.

"I'm sorry about that," Mia whispered.

"For what?"

"For making it awkward."

"It wasn't awkward," I said quickly. "It was just unexpected."

She smiled softly. "I like the unexpected."

I swallowed. "Me too."

We stopped near the creek; the water moving lazily over stones.

"You don't have to..." I began.

"I know," she said. "I just wanted to."

I nodded, and we stood there listening.

A man walked his dog; a woman jogged past, and a kid on a bike nearly fell into the creek.

Nothing suspicious.

"I think Zara's right," I said eventually. "He's waiting."

"Or watching," Mia said.

I glanced around instinctively.

"Do you feel weird?" she asked.

"Define weird."

"Like more noticeable."

I thought about Toby's stare, Sam's panic, and Zara's warning.

"Yes," I admitted.

She nodded. "Me too."

We headed back to the picnic table as the sun climbed higher to regroup with the rest of the team.

Zara returned shortly after, notebook full of scribbles.

"No contact," she said. "No signals. No notes."

Sam looked disappointed. "That's anticlimactic."

"It's tension," Zara corrected. "And tension breaks people."

Toby raised his hand. "Question."

"Yes?"

"If siblings like each other—"

"They're not siblings," I snapped.

"—does that increase vulnerability?" Toby finished.

Zara blinked. Then sighed. "Emotionally, yes."

Sam groaned. "I knew it."

Mia bit her lip, glancing at me.

Zara closed her notebook.

"Here's the thing. Whoever's behind the notes thrives on control, fear, and isolation."

She looked at us carefully.

"What they don't like is connection."

I felt something click into place.

"So, us... liking each other..." I began.

"Might be dangerous," Zara said. "Or it might be exactly what they can't control."

Sam frowned. "I don't like that answer."

Zara shrugged. "I didn't say it was comfortable."

We packed up and left.

As we walked away from the park, Mia slowed her pace to match mine.

She didn't take my hand this time.

But our arms brushed.

And that was enough.

Behind us, Sam muttered to Toby, "We need new protocols."

Toby nodded gravely. "For the record, I am still eked."

I smiled to myself because even with watchers, notes, plans, and fear, something else was growing.

Something warmer, something human.

And whatever came next, I had a feeling it was going to notice that first.

CHAPTER 11

A Confession with a False Alarm

The unexpected development happened the following Tuesday.

Which, if you remember, are invisible days.

Beige days.

Days that aren't supposed to do *anything* dramatic at all. That's how they get you. They wait until you're relaxed and then drop a surprise like a banana peel under your brain.

I was at my locker 217, still rude, still dented, trying to remember whether Zara had said *observe without reacting* or *react without observing* (they sound similar if you're tired), when someone cleared their throat behind me.

Not a Sam-throat-clear, for those were loud and confident and usually followed by space facts.

This was small and careful.

I turned and saw that it was Madison Reed.

I knew her in the way you know people who exist in the same building as you but never in the same orbit.

Grade Three.

Short and she always wore cardigans even when it was hot. Had hair that never stayed in its ponytail for over ten minutes.

She was clutching the straps of her backpack as if they might float away.

"Hi, Leo," she said.

My brain did a quick inventory.

Madison Reed. Grade Three.

No known connection to notes, watchers, Zara, or space satellites.

"Hi," I said cautiously.

She inhaled deeply, as if she were about to jump into water.

"I need to tell you something," she said.

That sentence had officially ruined my week.

"Okay," I said. "You can tell me."

She looked around the corridor, even though no one was paying any attention to us. Ethan Clarke was busy trying to bounce a tennis ball off the lockers without getting caught. Mrs Calder was nowhere nearby.

"I left a note," Madison said.

Time slowed.

My heart jumped so hard it almost smacked my ribs on the way down.

"You left a note?" I repeated.

She nodded. Fast, a little too fast.

"Yes."

A thousand thoughts crashed into each other in my head.

Is someone else involved? Is this a new variable?

"That's interesting," I said carefully. "What kind of note?"

Madison's eyes lit up. "A warning one."

My stomach flipped.

"About...?" I prompted.

"You know," she said vaguely. "The stuff."

The stuff.

Classic.

"Okay," I said. "And where did you leave it?"

She hesitated. "In a place."

That wasn't great.

I tried again. "Madison, what colour was the paper?"

She didn't hesitate this time.

"Purple."

Something inside me went still. Not dramatic, not scared-still but certain still.

There had never been a purple note. There had been pink, yellow, blue, and white.

No purple, not once.

My excitement drained away, leaving behind something else — disappointment mixed with understanding.

"Oh," I said.

Madison smiled nervously. "I wanted to help."

There it was.

I glanced at her properly then.

The way she stood half-turned, like she was ready to run. The way she kept checking my face for reactions.

She wasn't dangerous; she was just lonely.

"Madison," I said gently, "why did you think it was me you should tell?"

She swallowed. "Because you're in the group."

I sighed internally.

Of course, she knew.

Groups are like smells. You don't see them, but everyone knows when one exists.

"And you want to be in it," I said.

She nodded. "I'm good at noticing things too."

I believed her.

That was the problem.

"Come with me," I said.

Her eyes widened. "Really?"

"Yes," I said. "But I need you to be honest."

"I can be honest," she said immediately.

We walked toward the fig tree near the oval, where Zara, Mia, Sam, and Toby were mid-discussion.

Sam spotted us first.

"Leo," he stage-whispered, "why is there a Grade Three following you?"

Madison stiffened.

Zara turned and took one look at Madison and frowned. "Who's this?"

"This," I said, "is Madison."

Madison waved. Too enthusiastically.

"And she says she left a note." I continued.

Everything stopped.

Mia blinked, Zara's eyes sharpened, Sam gasped like he'd been offered front-row tickets to chaos, and all Toby did was adjust his helmet.

Zara stepped forward. "What kind of note?"

"A warning," Madison said quickly. "I wanted to protect people."

Zara folded her arms. "What colour?"

Madison hesitated.

I watched her face change as she realised, too late, that this was a test.

"Purple," she said again, quieter now.

Zara didn't react immediately.

Then she sighed.

"There have been no purple notes," Zara said calmly.

Madison's shoulders slumped.

"I just wanted to help," she said, her voice cracking a little. "Everyone's whispering. And you all look important."

Sam softened instantly.

"Being important is mostly stressful," he said.

Toby nodded. "And confusing."

Mia stepped closer to Madison.

"It's okay to want to belong."

Madison looked at her, eyes shiny.

"You don't think I'm bad?"

"No," Mia said firmly. "I think you're brave for coming forward."

Zara studied Madison for a long moment, and then she surprised me.

"Why purple?" Zara asked.

Madison sniffed. "Because it's my favourite colour. And because it's not loud like pink or scary like yellow."

Zara nodded slowly. "That's interesting."

Sam leaned toward Toby. "I like her already."

Toby whispered back, "She lied, but with feelings."

Zara looked at me. "You realised immediately."

"Yes," I said. "But not because she lied."

"Why then?" Zara asked.

"Because she didn't know the rules," I said. "But she knew fear."

Zara considered that.

Madison stood still, as if she were waiting to be dismissed.

Instead, Zara spoke.

"You're in Grade Three," Zara said.

"Yes," Madison whispered.

"That means," Zara continued, "you are officially too young to be involved in any dangerous plans."

Madison nodded. "Okay."

"But it also means you hear things older kids forget younger kids can hear." Zara added.

Madison looked up.

Zara met her gaze. "If we let you help, would you listen?"

Madison nodded so hard her ponytail nearly escaped.

"And would you tell the truth," Zara continued, "even if it meant not being included?"

Madison swallowed. "Yes."

Zara exhaled. "Then you're not a member."

Madison's face fell.

"You're an ally," Zara finished.

Madison froze.

"Ally?" she whispered.

Sam grinned. "It's like being important without meetings."

Toby nodded. "And fewer rules."

Madison smiled so wide it looked like it might hurt.

Zara held up a finger. "But there are conditions."

Madison stood straighter.

"No lying," Zara said. "No notes. No confrontations. You observe and report. To Leo."

Madison nodded furiously.

Zara glanced at me. "You vouch for her."

I hesitated for half a second, and then I nodded. "I do."

Madison looked at me as if I'd just handed her a medal.

As she walked away, lighter somehow, I felt something settle in my chest.

The watcher wanted isolation, control, and fear.

But what we were building accidentally, messily, with kissing witnesses and fake notes and Grade Three allies, was something else.

Connection.

And that, I realised, was the one thing you couldn't fake.

Not even with purple paper.

CHAPTER 12

Allies, Arithmetic, and a Serious Debate About Girls

Realising you have an ally is like realising you've been walking with one shoelace untied and no one told you, but instead of tripping, you suddenly start running better.

That afternoon, after Madison officially became an ally (capital A, invisible badge, no meetings), my brain wouldn't stop rearranging the idea. Allies meant eyes, ears, angles we didn't have. Allies meant the watcher had more variables to trip over.

Allies also meant people.

Which meant opinions.

And opinions meant meetings.

So, after school, I texted the group—which was now an actual thing I had saved in my phone as NOTES (NOT FOR NOTES)—and told everyone to meet behind the gym.

Sam arrived first, dragging Toby, who was eating something neon and unidentifiable.

Zara arrived next, notebook under her arm, already annoyed at something that hadn't happened yet. Mia came last, smiling when she saw me, which made my brain do that stupid warm flip again.

I had a feeling Sam had already figured something out, so I decided just to announce that we had a new ally.

"We have a new ally," I announced.

Sam gasped. "Is it Madison?"

"Yes."

Toby nodded approvingly. "She has strong honesty and resilience skills."

"She lied," Sam reminded him.

"Yes," Toby said, "but with remorse."

Zara crossed her arms. "Get to the point, Leo."

"The point," I said, "is that if one ally helped already, maybe more would help more."

Silence, then...

"No," Sam said immediately.

"Absolutely not," Toby added.

Zara blinked. "You didn't even hear the criteria."

Sam shook his head. "I've heard enough."

I frowned. "What do you mean?"

Toby leaned in, lowering his voice dramatically. "More girls."

Mia snorted.

Zara raised an eyebrow. "Is that a problem?"

"Yes," Sam and Toby said together.

"Explain," Zara said calmly, which is the scariest way anyone can say anything.

Sam cleared his throat. "Look. One girl liking one brother already caused consequences."

"That was one cheek," I muttered.

"ONE CHEEK TOO MANY," Sam said.

Toby nodded in agreement. "Yeah, consequences like emotional instability, handholding, and witness trauma."

Mia laughed openly now. "You two are ridiculous."

"Girls complicate missions," Sam said seriously.

"Boys complicate missions too, but in predictable ways."

"That's sexist," Zara said flatly.

Sam hesitated. "Is it?"

"Yes," Zara said.

"Oh," Sam said. "Okay. Still no."

I rubbed my forehead.

"This isn't about liking. It's about coverage."

"Coverage leads to conversations," Toby said.

"Then the conversations lead to feelings," Sam added.

"Then the feelings lead to kissing," Toby finished darkly.

Zara stared at them. "You two sound like grumpy old men trapped in small bodies."

Mia leaned closer to me. "I kind of love them."

I smiled. "They're exhausting."

"Okay," Zara said sharply. "Let's do this properly."

She opened her notebook and drew a quick grid.

"We need four more allies," she said.

Sam choked. "FOUR?"

"Yes," Zara said. "One for each zone we can't cover."

Toby squinted. "Zones?"

"Library," Zara said, ticking them off. "Hallways. Lunch area and the after-school exit."

Mia nodded. "That makes sense."

Sam frowned. "But why four girls?"

Zara looked up. "Who said girls?"

Sam brightened. "Oh. Boys are fine because boys are emotionally contained."

I coughed. "That's not—"

Zara closed the notebook with a snap. "They must be girls."

Dead silence.

Sam stared at her as if she'd just cancelled gravity.

"Why," he uttered, "would you say that?"

"Because boys are already watched differently and girls blend in more." Zara replied.

Zara continued. "They're less likely to be suspected of organising. Less likely to be challenged for being in places. Less likely to be dismissed as threatening."

Sam opened his mouth, closed it, then opened it again.

"That feels unfair," he said.

"Yes," Zara replied. "That's the point."

Toby looked torn. "But bringing in more girls presents a kissing risk. Look at those two," looking at Mia and me.

"Toby, you need to understand, we are recruiting observation allies, not recruiting romance." Zara explained.

I raised my hand slightly. "I agree with Zara."

Sam groaned. "Of course you do."

"Leo is compromised," Toby whispered.

"I am not compromised," I protested.

"You smiled," Sam said.

"That's my face."

Zara ignored us all.

"Alright, Zara, do you have any suggestions who these might be?" Mia asked.

"I do," and she flipped the page.

"Maya," she said. "Quiet. Always in the library. Notices everything."

Mia nodded. "Good listener."

"Jasmine," Zara continued. "Drama club. Excellent at pretending. Also overhears everything."

Sam frowned. "She sings."

"Undercover," Zara said.

"Chloe," Mia added. "She sits near the office. Always drawing. Adults forget she's there."

Zara nodded. "Good."

"And Taylor," I said, surprising myself. "She's new. Still invisible."

Zara looked at me thoughtfully. "Good catch."

Sam stared at the list. "That's all, girls."

"Yes," Zara said.

Sam exhaled. "Sorry, Toby."

Toby slumped. "Sorry, Sam."

They shook hands solemnly.

"So, what's the plan?" Mia asked.

Zara smiled slightly. "We don't recruit them."

I blinked. "We don't?"

"No," Zara said. "We let them recruit themselves."

I leaned forward. "How?"

Zara tapped her pen.

"We make ourselves visible. Just enough. Let curiosity do the work."

Sam frowned. "That sounds like flirting."

"It's not," Zara said. "It's signalling."

Toby brightened. "Signals I understand."

"We'll create situations, you know, moments," Zara continued. "Conversations that feel accidental. Overheard questions. Observations that invite a response."

Mia smiled. "Like Madison."

"Yes," Zara said. "Honesty attracts honesty."

I felt something settle again. The plan felt right.

"So," Sam said reluctantly, "no kissing?"

Mia laughed. "No promises."

Sam groaned. "We're doomed."

As we packed up, I looked at the list again.

Maya. Jasmine. Chloe. Taylor.

Four more allies, four more perspectives.

And for the first time, I realised something important: we weren't just building a plan; we were building a network.

And whatever, or whoever, was leaving notes was about to discover the one thing they hadn't accounted for.

People who chose each other.

Even when it was messy, even when it involved girls.

Especially then.

CHAPTER 13

How to be Obvious Without Looking Like You Are Trying

If you ever need proof that being subtle is harder than it looks, try doing it on purpose.

That was the lesson of Monday.

We arrived at school with a plan; well, it was Zara's plan, which meant it had rules, layers, and a very specific definition of "casual."

The idea was simple in theory: be visible in the right places, say the right half-things, and let curiosity do the rest.

No recruiting speeches, no secret handshakes, and no notes.

"Think of it like leaving breadcrumbs," Zara had said.

Sam immediately imagined pigeons.

"Breadcrumbs attract birds," he'd warned. "And birds are unpredictable."

"Focus," Zara had replied, which is what she said to everyone when she didn't want to argue with Sam.

So, we split up, each of us assigned a location and a tone. Zara took the library. Mia took the art room corridor. Sam and Toby were told to "exist loudly" near the lockers. I was assigned the benches near the office, which Zara called "high-traffic, low-suspicion."

It sounded very professional.

I felt nine and underqualified.

I sat on the bench and pretended to tie my shoelaces for a full three minutes. People walked past. Teachers nodded. The office door opened and closed. I waited for something to happen. Nothing did.

"Maybe we're doing it wrong," Sam whispered loudly as he passed Toby, both of them pretending to look for a lost pencil.

"You're not supposed to whisper loudly," I muttered.

"That's my whisper," Sam said.

Then Chloe walked by.

She was holding a sketchbook and humming softly, eyes down, hair falling in her face. She paused when she saw me, then smiled politely.

"Hi," she said.

"Hi," I said, which was becoming a recurring problem.

She glanced at my shoelaces. "You dropped something."

I looked down, but nothing had been dropped.

"Oh," I said quickly. "Yeah. I mean—no. I was just... tying."

She nodded, as if this made perfect sense. "I like your shoes."

"Thanks," I said. "They're shoes."

She laughed, a quick, surprised sound.

"Are you waiting for someone?" she asked.

This was it. Breadcrumb time.

"Kind of," I said. "We're talking about school stuff."

Her eyes flicked toward the office door, then back to me. "What kind of school stuff?"

I shrugged. "The kind you notice when you sit near here."

She considered that, then smiled again.

"Yeah. You notice a lot from here."

She walked on, but slower.

And when she did, she glanced back once.

Breadcrumb number one: placed.

At recess, Mia had better luck.

I found her near the art room, leaning against the wall while Jasmine dramatically retold a story involving glitter, a broken prop, and "emotional betrayal."

"I just think," Jasmine was saying, "that if you're going to borrow someone's feather boa, you should emotionally prepare them."

Mia nodded sympathetically. "That's fair."

Jasmine noticed me watching and waved. "Leo, right?"

I blinked. "Uh, yeah."

She grinned. "You look like someone who overhears things."

"I—what?"

She leaned closer.

"People talk when they think you're not listening."

Mia hid a smile.

"Do they?" I said.

"Oh, yes," Jasmine said. "Especially near the lockers."

She swept away dramatically, leaving behind a faint smell of hairspray and possibility.

Breadcrumb number two: scattered flamboyantly.

The real test came at lunch.

Zara had positioned herself in the library like a statue, reading the same page of a book for twenty minutes. Maya sat two tables away, quietly eating an apple and reading something thick and serious.

I approached carefully.

"Is that good?" I asked, gesturing to her book.

She looked up, surprised. "It's interesting."

"That's code for 'yes, but it hurts,'" I said.

She smiled slightly. "Pretty much."

I sat. "I'm Leo."

"Maya," she said. "You're involved in something."

Not a question.

My heart skipped. "Why do you say that?"

"You watch people when you think they're not watching you," she said. "That usually means you're looking for patterns."

I stared. "Do I?"

"Yes," she said calmly. "You also listen to footsteps."

I glanced down. "Okay. That's unsettling."

She shrugged. "Observation is contagious."

Breadcrumb number three: devoured thoughtfully.

By the end of the day, we regrouped behind the gym, buzzing with half-successes and almosts.

"Well?" Sam demanded.

Zara closed her notebook. "We wait."

"That's it?" Toby asked.

"That's it," Zara said. "If they're interested, they'll come to us."

"And if they're not?" Sam asked.

"Then we don't force it," Mia said.

Sam frowned. "I don't like waiting."

"No one does," Zara replied. "That's why it works."

On Tuesday, it worked, and Chloe found me first.

She sat beside me on the bench, sketchbook open, pencil moving.

"I draw what I hear," she said casually.

"That sounds impossible."

She shrugged. "You'd be surprised."

She turned the sketchbook toward me.

It wasn't a picture of me. Or the bench.

It was the office door. And around it—little arrows. Times. Notes.

My stomach flipped.

"You've noticed," I said quietly.

She nodded. "I didn't know if it mattered."

"It does," I said.

She smiled, relieved.

Jasmine arrived next, flopping down dramatically.

"So," she said, "hypothetically, if someone wanted to help with a secret-but-not-illegal thing, how would one go about that?"

Mia laughed. "Hypothetically?"

"Obviously," Jasmine said. "I'm very ethical."

Maya came last, slipping into the circle without a word.

"I think someone's trying to scare people," she said. "And I don't like it."

Zara watched them all, eyes sharp but satisfied.

Sam whispered to Toby, "They came to us."

Toby nodded. "Breadcrumbs."

We didn't make speeches. We didn't swear oaths.

We just told the truth.

About notes, about watching, about being careful, about why we needed help, and they listened.

When the bell rang, none of us moved right away.

It felt as if something had shifted.

Not loudly. Not obviously. But enough.

As we walked home, Mia bumped my shoulder gently.

"That went well," she said.

"Yeah," I said. "It did."

Behind us, Sam sighed dramatically. "Okay. I admit it."

"What?" I asked.

"Girls are effective," he said. "But still, eek."

Toby nodded. "Strategically valuable. Emotionally alarming."

I laughed.

Because for the first time since the pink note fell from my locker, I wasn't just reacting anymore; we had a plan; we had people, and whoever thought they could control us with paper and fear were about to learn something very important.

You can't watch everyone, not when everyone is watching back.

CHAPTER 14

The Quiet Before Someone Blinks

Something changed after that. Not loudly. No alarms. No notes fluttered to the floor. No dramatic confrontations behind the gym.

Just quiet.

Too quiet.

The new allies didn't rush in or start whispering in corners. Maya read. Jasmine performed at normal levels of drama. Chloe drew. Taylor, who we'd quietly looped in during science, mostly observed like she was filing everything away for later.

And the notes?

Nothing. No colours, no warnings, and no; *Stop looking*.

At first, that felt like relief then it felt like a held breath.

I noticed it on Thursday afternoon while sitting at my desk, pretending to do homework and actually listening to the house settle around me.

Sam was building something noisy out of Lego.

Mum was on the phone while Dad was humming off-key while fixing a cupboard hinge that probably didn't need fixing.

Normal sounds.

But underneath them was something else.

Anticipation.

The kind that prickles at the back of your neck when you know someone is waiting for you to make a mistake.

At school the next day, Zara confirmed it.

"They're testing us. Silence is a tactic." She whispered as we stood near the library shelves.

"To make us doubt ourselves," Mia added.

"To make us relax," I finished.

Sam leaned in. "I am not relaxed."

"Good," Zara said. "Stay that way."

At lunch, Madison passed me a folded piece of paper.

My heart jumped—then settled.

It was white. Unwritten.

A warning without words.

I folded it back and handed it to her.

"Something's coming," I said.

She nodded. "I feel it too."

As the bell rang, I caught my reflection in a window.

I looked the same. But I wasn't.

Whatever this was, whatever the watcher was planning, I knew one thing for certain: they were going to blink, and when they did.

We'd be watching.

CHAPTER 15

The One Who Didn't Belong

We stopped calling him *whoever's leaving the notes*. That name was too long, too polite, too unsure.

By Thursday afternoon, after a ten-minute discussion behind the gym that involved Zara pacing, Sam doodling surveillance cones, and Mia biting her thumbnail like she was trying not to say something important too early, we had a new name.

The Watcher.

Not because it sounded scary, though it did, but because it sounded *accurate*.

"He watches patterns," Zara said. "Not people. People are just... part of the pattern."

"And patterns don't have feelings," Sam added helpfully.

"Which makes him rude," Toby said.

"But also predictable," Mia said.

That was the part that stuck predictability.

By process of elimination, we'd crossed Mr Bell off the list.

Not because he was innocent in the heroic, movie-ending way. But because he was sloppy, too obvious, too pleased with himself when confronted.

Mr Bell enjoyed being *seen* as mysterious.

He liked power that showed.

The Watcher didn't.

"The Watcher doesn't want attention," I said. "He wants influence."

Zara nodded. "Which means he wouldn't risk being seen near the school too often."

"And if the notes stopped," Mia said quietly, "it means he moved."

That was when it clicked.

"Not *into* the school," I said slowly. "Out of it."

Zara's eyes sharpened. "You think he's nearby."

"In the neighbourhood," I said. "Close enough to watch routines. Close enough to learn patterns. Far enough to stay invisible."

Sam's eyes lit up. "Stakeout."

Zara sighed. "Absolutely not—"

"Stakeout," Sam repeated, louder.

"—you're seven—"

"Stakeout," Toby whispered reverently.

Mia looked at me. "You're thinking of the school path."

I nodded. The school path wasn't technically part of the school. It cut through a strip of public land—trees, uneven grass, a bench with graffiti that said *L + K 4EVER,* even though no one knew who L and K were anymore. Parents used it. Dog walkers. People who lived nearby and didn't want to walk the long way around. People who could watch without looking like they were watching.

Zara folded her arms. "I don't like it."

"I know," I said.

"But" she continued, "I don't have proof to stop you."

Sam beamed. "Stakeout."

The plan was simple, too simple, which made it dangerous.

After school, Sam and I would "walk home slowly." Which, for Sam, was already an achievement. We'd break off near the maple tree, the big one near the bend in the path, with a trunk so wide three kids couldn't wrap their arms around it. We would hide, we would watch, and we would count people.

No phones, no notes, no bait, just our eyes.

Mia wanted to come.

Zara said no.

"Too many variables," Zara said. "If someone sees a group of kids hiding, that's suspicious. Two brothers loitering is just unfortunate."

Sam took that as a compliment, and I was impressed with how Zara thought.

When the bell rang, my heart started pounding in a slow, heavy way that felt like it was knocking from the inside.

We walked at a normal pace, well, mostly.

Sam kicked stones and talked about how maple trees produced helicopters and how helicopters were a very inefficient way to travel unless you were evacuating a volcano.

I nodded as if I were listening until we reached the tree.

Sam pretended to retie his shoe, and I pretended to help.

Then we slipped behind the trunk.

The bark was rough against my back and the sap smell. Leaves overhead whispered as if they knew something we didn't.

"Okay," Sam whispered. "Rules."

"No talking," I whispered back.

"Breathing?"

"Yes."

"Blinking?"

"Preferably."

We waited.

The first people came through in clusters.

Kids with parents. Loud, loose, relieved. Backpacks swinging. Laughter spilling everywhere. A mum arguing gently with a kid about homework. A dad on his phone. Normal.

Normal was boring.

I counted silently.

One, two, three, a man with a dog. The dog sniffed the tree. I froze, and Sam froze.

The dog sneezed and moved on, and my heart restarted.

A woman pushing a pram, a teenage boy on his bike, and a delivery driver checking an address and muttering.

Normal, and then the flow slowed, the noise faded, and it felt like the air changed.

It's hard to explain how you can feel that seeing nothing different, but you can. The way the world pauses before something happens.

Like a held breath.

Sam felt it too. I could tell because he stopped moving entirely.

Footsteps.

One set; slow, measured, not rushed, not wandering.

Purposeful.

I leaned forward slightly, peering around the edge of the trunk.

She came into view.

She wasn't a teacher.

That was the first thing I knew for sure.

Teachers carried themselves in a certain way, even when they were off duty. A stiffness, a look of being used to being watched, and this woman didn't have that.

She walked as if she didn't expect anyone to look at her.

She was in her late thirties, maybe early forties. I don't know – kind of hard to tell with adults.

Brown coat, a scarf wrapped loosely., her hair pulled back, but not tightly. With no bag, no dog, and no phone in her hand.

She slowed as she reached the bend in the path.

Stopped.

My breath caught.

She turned.

Not all the way. Just enough to look *back* toward the school gates.

She stood there still for a full five seconds.

Watching, not scanning, not glancing, but watching.

Sam's fingers dug into my sleeve.

"Leo," he breathed. "She's not normal."

I didn't answer.

The woman tilted her head slightly, as if she were listening for something.

Then she smiled. It wasn't a big smile, not friendly but not mean, but it looked like *knowing*.

She reached into her coat pocket.

My heart slammed.

Phone? A notebook? Maybe a camera?

She pulled out nothing, just her hand.

She looked down at it, flexed her fingers once, then slipped it back into her pocket.

Then she walked on.

Past the maple tree.

Close enough that I could smell her perfume—something sharp and clean, not sweet.

She didn't look at us.

Not once.

Which meant she didn't need to.

I stayed frozen until her footsteps faded completely.

Then Sam exploded into movement.

"DID YOU SEE THAT," he hissed, eyes huge. "DID YOU SEE HOW SHE STOOD?"

"Yes," I whispered.

"She stopped."

"Yes."

"She smiled at the school."

"Yes."

"She was alone. She didn't have a kid, or a dog, or shopping." Sam added.

"No," I said.

"Leo," Sam said slowly, "she's a Watcher."

I swallowed.

"Maybe," I said. "Or maybe she's just nearby."

Sam stared at me. "You don't believe that."

"No," I admitted. "I don't."

We waited another ten minutes.

No one else unusual came through.

Which somehow made it worse.

At home, I barely tasted dinner, and Sam barely breathed.

We didn't say anything in front of Mum and Dad. Not because we were told not to—but because something in both of us knew this was bigger now.

Later, in our room, Sam sat cross-legged on his bed, helmet on even though it was bedtime.

"She knew," he said.

"Knew what?"

"That she was being watched."

I shook my head. "She didn't look surprised."

"Exactly," Sam said. "She expected it."

I lay back, staring at the ceiling stars.

"She didn't belong," I said.

Sam nodded. "That's how you know."

The next morning, I told the group.

Every detail, every second.

The stopping, how she looked, and that smile.

Zara went still.

"A woman," she said. "Not connected to the school."

Mia's face was pale. "Did she see you?"

"No," I said. "But she didn't need to."

Zara closed her notebook slowly. "That changes things."

"How?" Sam asked.

"Because," Zara said, "schools are predictable. Neighbourhoods are not."

Toby swallowed. "What does that mean?"

"It means," Zara replied, "the Watcher isn't hiding behind rules anymore."

Mia looked at me. "Do you think she knows about us?"

I thought of the smile.

"Yes," I said.

"And?" Mia asked.

I exhaled slowly.

"I think," I said, "she's been watching longer than we thought."

No one spoke after that.

Somewhere between the maple tree and that quiet smile, the game had changed.

And the scariest part?

For the first time, the Watcher wasn't invisible anymore.

She was real.

And she was close.

CHAPTER 16

The Inside Person

The thing about big discoveries is that they don't always arrive with fireworks. Sometimes they arrive with crumbs in your lap and a juice box straw that won't work because it's been stabbed through the wrong side.

It was lunchtime. I was sitting on the low brick wall near the gardens—the one that looked out over the oval and the lunch tables. Mia sat close enough that our shoulders almost touched, which made everything feel both calmer and louder at the same time.

I was pretending to eat my sandwich while Mia was pretending not to notice that I was pretending.

Zara was across the yard, under the shade of the fig tree, notebook open, scanning as if she was counting invisible things. Chloe was sketching. Maya was reading. Jasmine was doing something dramatic with a group of girls that involved hand gestures and a voice that could probably be heard from space.

Everything looked normal.

But none of it felt normal anymore.

Because I couldn't stop thinking about the woman on the path. The way she'd paused. The way she'd smiled toward the school, as if it belonged to her, as if she'd already won.

Mia nudged my knee gently with hers.

"You're doing the staring thing," she said.

"I'm thinking," I muttered.

"That's the same thing," she replied.

I opened my mouth to say something smart, like *Thinking is just staring with purpose,* but before I could, Sam and Toby appeared.

Not walked. Not approached. Rushed.

Sam's face was bright with the excitement that usually meant someone had said the word "meteor." Toby's helmet was crooked, which was basically the emergency siren version of Toby.

They skidded to a stop in front of us.

Sam put both hands on his knees, panting like he'd sprinted through an asteroid field.

"Leo," he gasped, "we have…"

"A development," Toby finished, voice trembling with importance.

Mia sat up straighter. "What is it?"

Sam didn't answer immediately.

He looked at me like I was about to be proud of him, and it made my stomach twist because I suddenly realised, he'd been thinking harder than I had, and I hated that, but also, I loved it.

Sam pointed dramatically toward the school buildings as if presenting evidence in court.

"Leo," he announced, loud enough that a few kids nearby turned, "the Watcher has to have an accomplice."

I blinked.

"A what?"

"An inside person," Toby said quickly, nodding as if this was obvious. "A school-level operative."

Sam waved his hands. "How was she getting the notes into the school? She would've been spotted. Adults don't walk into school as if they're invisible. People notice."

My brain stalled, then restarted, and then sprinted.

I stared at Sam.

Mia stared at Sam.

We both looked at each other.

And in that moment, I felt something awful and hilarious at the same time.

How did we not think of that? How did *Zara* not think of that?

The whole time we'd been arguing about Mr Bell and maps and bait and silent tactics, we'd been acting like the Watcher was a magician—appearing, disappearing, slipping notes through walls.

But she wasn't magic; she was method, and method needed access.

Inside access.

My sandwich slid slightly in my hand. I didn't care.

Mia's mouth was open. She closed it and then opened it again.

"Sam," she said slowly, "that is actually really smart."

Sam's chest puffed out like he'd just been awarded a medal.

"Thank you," he said. "I know, but Toby helped as well."

I rubbed my forehead.

"Wait," I said, "say it again. Explain it."

Sam looked offended, as if I'd asked him to prove gravity.

"Okay," he said more calmly. "The Watcher is a woman. She's outside. Neighbourhood. Path. Creepy smile. Fine. But the notes were inside the school. In lockers. In desk trays. In a lunchbox once."

Mia shuddered.

"You can't do that from outside," Sam continued. "Not unless you're a ninja."

Toby nodded gravely. "Or a ghost."

"Or" Sam said, holding up a finger, "someone inside the school is doing the delivering."

Silence and even the playground noise seemed to dip for a second, like the idea had sucked the air out of everything.

I looked over toward Zara.

She was still by the fig tree, writing something in her notebook.

Totally calm. On top of things, except maybe not this.

Or maybe she had thought of it and hadn't told us. Because Zara sometimes acted as if information was a currency and she was the bank.

Mia leaned closer to me, voice low. "If Sam's right, it means we're dealing with two people."

"Or more," I whispered back.

Toby leaned in too, like we were a tiny huddle of disaster.

"And" Toby added, "the inside person has to be someone who can move around without suspicion."

My stomach tightened again.

"An adult," I said quietly.

Sam nodded. "Exactly."

Mia's eyes went wide. "But who?"

"Teacher?" Toby suggested.

"Office staff, or a parent volunteer, or a student," Mia whispered.

We all froze.

Because that was a possibility too, wasn't it?

A student could slip notes into lockers, into desk trays, even lunchboxes.

But a student wouldn't have been able to access every place without getting noticed. And the notes weren't sloppy. They were deliberate. Planned.

I felt the weight of the white warning note in my memory.

Be careful.

A leak.

A second-hand in the system.

But was the leak the accomplice?

Or was the leaker trying to stop the accomplice?

My head hurt from all the layers.

I stood abruptly.

Mia grabbed my sleeve. "Leo?"

"I need Zara," I said.

Sam looked proud. "Yes. Bring in command."

We walked fast across the yard.

Sam and Toby followed like two eager satellites, bumping into each other once and then pretending it was on purpose.

Zara looked up as we approached.

Her eyes flicked from my face to Sam's to Toby's.

"You've got that look," she said. "The one that means you're about to say something I already know or something I should've known."

Sam raised his hand. "We think the Watcher has an accomplice."

Zara didn't blink. She just went still. That was when I knew Sam wasn't just right; he was *dangerously* right.

Zara closed her notebook slowly.

"How did you get there?" she asked, voice calm but sharp.

Sam launched into his explanation again, with Toby adding words like "operative" and "infiltration" that he absolutely didn't understand but enjoyed saying.

Zara listened without interrupting.

When Sam finished, Zara nodded once.

"I considered it," she said.

My stomach sank. "You did?"

"Yes," she said. "But I didn't have enough evidence to say it out loud."

Mia frowned. "Why not?"

Zara's eyes flicked across the yard, scanning faces.

"Because the second you say *inside person,* everyone becomes a suspect," she said quietly. "And panic makes people sloppy."

Sam looked annoyed. "But we need to know."

"Yes," Zara said. "We do."

Toby leaned in. "So, who is it?"

Zara exhaled slowly.

"That's the problem," she said. "It could be someone with access and motive."

"Motive," I repeated.

Because that was the part that made my skin crawl.

Why would anyone, adult, or kid, do this?

Why would they help a woman who watched the school as if it were a stage?

Zara's gaze landed on me.

"We have to ask the question we've been avoiding," she said.

Mia swallowed. "Which is?"

Zara spoke softly, as if the words were sharp.

"Why us?"

No one answered.

Sam's bravado faded a little.

Toby's helmet tilted as if even it was listening harder.

I stared across the oval at the groups of kids—laughing, chasing, eating, living in ignorance.

Why *us*?

Why Mia, who found the shoebox?

Why me, the kid with the stubborn locker and the habit of looking?

Why the warning note?

Why the silence tactic?

And now, why the woman outside?

Zara tapped her notebook.

"We know the Watcher watches patterns. We know notes are about control. We know control needs access."

She looked at each of us.

"So," she said, "we find the access points."

Mia nodded. "Teachers' lounge. Office. Duty rosters."

"Caretaker's areas," I added.

Sam raised a hand. "Also, the photocopier room."

Zara blinked. "Why the photocopier room?"

Sam shrugged. "It's always humming. Humming hides footsteps."

Toby nodded as if this made perfect sense. "Also, paper lives there."

Zara looked like she wanted to roll her eyes but couldn't argue with "paper lives there."

"Fine," she said. "Access points."

Mia's voice was small. "And the why?"

Zara's expression softened, just slightly.

"That might come later," she said. "Or it might be the first thing we discover. Motive leaks through behaviour."

I swallowed.

Sam tugged my sleeve. "Leo."

"What?"

Sam's eyes were serious now, not excited.

"If she has an inside person," he said, "then she's not just watching the school."

He glanced toward the street beyond the oval, toward the path where we'd seen her.

"She's watching *who goes in and out.*"

My stomach dropped.

Because I knew what he was saying.

If she could watch entrances... and had someone inside...then she could watch *us.*

Not just our lockers, not just our desks, but our routines, our exits, our walking paths, and our homes.

Mia's fingers found my hand without thinking.

I held on.

Zara's voice cut through the fear.

"Listen," she said. "We don't panic. We don't accuse. We stay smart."

She flipped to a fresh page in her notebook.

"Tonight," Zara continued, "everyone writes everything they know about adult movement in the school. Who's where. When? Which doors are used? Who has the keys?"

Sam whispered to Toby, "Keys. Classic."

"And tomorrow," Zara said, "we compare notes."

I almost laughed at the word *notes* and then didn't because it felt wrong.

As the bell rang and the kids packed up, I felt the world bend slightly.

Not because something had happened. Because something had been *revealed*.

The Watcher wasn't a single shadow.

She was a system, and systems didn't just happen they were built by someone for a reason.

As we walked away, Mia squeezed my fingers once.

"Sam saved us," she whispered.

I glanced back at my little brother, who was walking with Toby as if they'd just discovered fire.

"He did," I agreed.

And as scary as it was, there was one thing I couldn't ignore anymore: The Watcher had an inside person.

Which meant the game wasn't just on the path, it was also inside the school, right under our noses.

CHAPTER 17

Narrowing It Down

Saturday arrived as it always did—quiet on the surface, noisy underneath. The park looked harmless enough. Kids on bikes. A dad threw a tennis ball to a dog that clearly preferred sticks. The old rotunda cast its round shadow as it had done a thousand times before.

But for us, the park wasn't a park anymore.

It was neutral ground.

We gathered near the maple tree—the same one Sam and I had used as a cover for our stakeout. I noticed that immediately, and so did Sam. He patted the trunk once, affectionately, as if it was an old friend who'd kept a secret.

My little brother is a bit weird.

Zara arrived first, notebook tucked under her arm, expression already in *focus mode*. Mia came with Madison trailing behind her, trying very hard to look invisible and failing completely. Chloe and Maya sat on the grass nearby, sketchbook and book in hand respectively, both of them watching without appearing to. Jasmine swept in late, apologising loudly for reasons no one asked about. Taylor slipped in quietly, almost unnoticed.

Sam and Toby plopped down opposite Zara like they were attending a very serious summit. Toby had removed his helmet, which meant things were *extremely* serious.

Zara clapped once.

"Okay," she said. "This is not a guessing game."

Sam raised his hand. "Can it be a *little* bit of a guessing game?"

"No," Zara replied.

He lowered his hand. "Okay."

Zara opened her notebook. "We know there is at least one inside person. Someone who can move through the school unnoticed. Someone who can place notes without triggering attention."

"And someone with access to paper," Toby added.

"Yes," Zara said. "Paper is key."

I nodded. "And timing. The notes appeared when the classrooms were empty. During transitions. Lunch. After school."

Mia hugged her knees. "Which means whoever it is understands school rhythms."

"Or works inside them," Maya said quietly.

Everyone looked at her.

She shrugged. "Patterns repeat. Adults rely on that."

Zara nodded approvingly. "Exactly."

She drew a line down the page.

"We are not accusing," she continued. "We are observing. Today we create a *shortlist*."

"Shortlists are scary," Sam muttered.

"Necessary," Zara replied.

She looked up at us. "Five suspects. No names outside this group, no confronting, no spreading."

Madison raised her hand timidly. "Do we write them down?"

Zara smiled slightly. "You can. Just not where anyone can see."

She turned the notebook around so that we could all see the page.

Suspect One: Mrs Calder

I swallowed when Zara wrote the name.

Mrs Calder. My teacher.

"Why her?" Mia asked softly.

Zara tapped the page. "She has constant access to lockers, desk trays, and students' belongings. She knows everyone's habits."

"And" Sam added, "she has eyebrows that could deliver threats."

"That is not evidence," Mia said.

"It's *supporting detail*," Sam replied.

I frowned. "She's strict, but she's also fair."

Zara nodded. "Which makes her unlikely. But not impossible."

Chloe spoke up. "She's always in the building late."

That made my stomach twist.

Zara wrote: *Access, authority, predictable movements.*

Suspect Two: Mr Bell (Caretaker)

Sam leaned forward eagerly. "I knew he'd be back."

Zara sighed. "He was ruled out as the Watcher. That doesn't mean he's not involved."

"Or being used," Mia said.

"Yes," Zara agreed. "He has the keys. He moves everywhere. He knows which areas are empty."

"And he enjoys feeling important," Sam added.

Toby nodded. "Power-adjacent individuals often cooperate."

Zara wrote five words: *keys, mobility, and manipulation.*

I felt uneasy. Mr Bell annoyed me, but the idea that he might help someone else was worse than the idea he was acting alone.

Suspect Three: Mrs Dalloway (Librarian)

Jasmine gasped softly. "She knows *everything.*"

Zara nodded. "She controls a quiet space. Students trust her. Adults overlook her."

"And" Sam said, "books hide paper."

Zara paused, then added that.

Maya frowned. "She notices when people don't return books. She notices patterns."

"That can go either way," Mia said. "Protective or controlling."

Zara wrote: *Observation. Trust. Access to students across grades.*

Suspect Four: Office Volunteer (Mrs Henley)

This one made everyone shift.

Mrs Henley wasn't a teacher. She worked part time in the office. Handed out notes. Called parents. Sorted mail.

"She touches paper all day," I said quietly.

"And she knows who's absent," Chloe added. "And when rooms are empty."

"And" Taylor said for the first time, "she's always smiling. Even when kids are crying."

That made the air feel colder.

Zara nodded. "Smiling can be disarming."

Sam swallowed. "That's creepy."

Zara wrote: *Paper flow. Information hub. Gatekeeper role.*

Suspect Five: A student (unknown)

This one felt different.

Zara didn't write a name.

Just: *student accomplice.*

"A student could place notes without suspicion," Mia said slowly.

"And wouldn't raise alarms being near lockers," I added.

"But" Sam said, "why would a student help a grown-up?"

Everyone went quiet. That was the question, wasn't it?

Zara finally spoke. "Control. Attention. Or fear."

Madison hugged her arms. "What if they were told to?"

I thought of the white note.

Be careful.

A warning, or perhaps regret, with Zara writing in her notes: *Motivation unknown. Likely pressure or reward.*

She closed the notebook.

"These are our five," she said. "No one else."

Sam frowned. "That's still a lot."

"Yes," Zara agreed. "So, we narrow again."

"How?" Mia asked.

"By behaviour," Zara replied. "We watch for changes. For stress. For disruption in routine."

Toby raised a finger.

"People who stop being predictable."

Zara nodded. "Exactly."

I looked around the group.

Mia, Zara, Sam, Toby, Chloe, Maya, Jasmine, Taylor, and Madison.

So many eyes now, and so many angles.

And suddenly, for the first time since this started, I felt something shift in our favour.

"They can't watch all of us," I said.

Zara met my eyes. "No. They can't."

Sam grinned. "Especially not if we're annoying."

"Please don't be annoying to adults," Mia said.

Sam thought. "Okay. Selectively annoying."

As the meeting wrapped up, the park returned to normal around us. Dogs barked. A kid fell off a scooter and got back up. Life continued.

But underneath it all, something had changed again.

We weren't chasing shadows anymore; we had names; we had roles; and we had patterns.

And somewhere inside the school, or just beyond it, someone realised that the quiet game they'd been playing was getting crowded.

As we packed up, I glanced once more at the path beyond the trees.

No woman in a brown coat, no smile, but I knew better now.

She didn't need to be there.

Not when she had someone inside.

And whoever that was, they were running out of places to hide.

CHAPTER 18

The Suspects

We divided the suspects the way adults divide chores—carefully, with logic, and pretending feelings weren't involved.

Which, of course, meant feelings were *absolutely* involved.

The park table was chipped and covered in old scratches, initials carved into the wood by kids who'd come before us and thought their names needed to last forever. Zara stood at the head of it like she owned the place, notebook open, pencil hovering just above the page as if the wrong movement might set something off.

She had written nothing yet.

That was how I knew this part mattered.

"Okay," she said. "We don't rush this."

Sam immediately rocked back on his heels. "I hate sentences that start like that."

Zara ignored him.

She scanned our faces one by one, as if she were measuring a weight we didn't know we were carrying. Mia sat straighter than usual. Chloe hugged her sketchbook to her chest. Maya watched quietly, eyes flicking between Zara's pencil and the page. Madison lingered just behind Mia, hands clasped, trying to take up as little space as possible. Toby stood beside Sam, helmet under one arm like he'd removed it out of respect.

Then Zara looked at me.

"Mrs Calder," she said.

Just my teacher's name.

Nothing else.

My stomach dipped so fast it felt like I'd missed a step on the stairs.

"I get my teacher," I said.

It came out flatter than I meant it to, like I'd already accepted it even though I hadn't. Mrs Calder. The person who handed back my tests. The person who knew my handwriting. The person who could tell when I wasn't listening, even when I pretended, I was.

"Yes," Zara replied calmly. "You're already inside her orbit. That gives you cover."

I nodded, even though the word *orbit* made me feel like I was about to be flung into space without a helmet.

"And trauma," Sam added helpfully.

I shot him a look. "You are not helping."

"I'm adding realism," he said.

Zara didn't even sigh this time. She just made a small mark next to my name in her notebook, like she'd mentally ticked a box labelled *Leo: emotionally compromised but useful*.

"Mia," Zara said, shifting her gaze.

Mia straightened immediately, as if she were responding to a call only, she could hear.

"Mrs Henley is mine," Mia said before Zara could finish.

Her voice was steady, but I saw the way her shoulders squared, the way she inhaled like she was bracing herself. Mrs Henley—the office, the forms, the paper trail that touched everything.

Zara studied her for a second. "You're sure?"

Mia nodded. "I can do it."

There was something fierce in her eyes then, something quiet but solid. I felt that familiar warmth in my chest and pushed it down. This wasn't the time.

Zara nodded. "Alright. Librarian for me."

She wrote *Mrs Dalloway* in neat, controlled letters.

"That tracks," Jasmine murmured. "She sees *everything*."

"And no one ever notices her noticing," Maya added.

Zara didn't comment. She just underlined the name once.

Then, Sam and Toby raised their hands together.

Perfectly in sync.

"Mr Bell," they said in unison.

Zara closed her eyes.

Not dramatically. Not annoyed.

Briefly. Like someone counting to three.

"This," she said carefully, opening them again, "is why I didn't want to assign him to you."

Sam beamed. "We're uniquely qualified."

"At annoying adults," Toby added earnestly.

"Exactly," Sam said, nodding as if this was a badge of honour.

Zara pressed her lips together. "You realise this is a *serious* investigation."

"Yes," Sam said. "And we take annoyance very seriously."

Toby nodded. "We specialise."

Zara exhaled through her nose. "Fine. But if you get detention—"

"We won't," Sam said quickly.

"If you *almost* get detention—"

"We'll retreat," Toby promised.

"If you provoke him—"

Sam held up a finger. "Define provoke."

Zara stared at him.

He lowered his hand.

"Okay," she said. "Assignments stand."

She tapped the notebook shut.

"And now we repeat the rules," she said. "Because someone always forgets."

Sam opened his mouth.

Zara raised an eyebrow.

He closed it again.

"No accusations," she said. "Not even implied ones."

"No confrontations," Mia added.

"No writing anything down where it could be found," Zara continued.

"No notes, no lists, no doodles that accidentally look like maps."

Sam glanced at the dirt near his shoes where he'd already drawn something suspiciously diagram-like and scuffed it out with his foot.

"And most importantly," Zara said, voice lowering slightly, "no acting like detectives."

That one hit harder than the rest.

I felt it in my chest.

Because we *felt* like detectives.

Like we were solving something important. Like we were smarter than the adults who hadn't noticed—or hadn't acted.

But that was the trap.

"We're just kids," Zara reminded us. "Being kids is the disguise. It should be what we do best."

I thought about that.

About how being a kid meant asking questions that didn't sound dangerous. Being in places without raising alarms. Being ignored when you wanted to be—and heard when you didn't expect it.

That part was easy, and the hard part was pretending not to care.

Sam rocked forward again. "What does 'being kids' actually look like?"

Zara considered. "It looks like homework questions. Lost items. Bathroom passes. Casual conversations."

"Annoying conversations," Sam clarified.

"Yes," Zara said. "Especially those."

Toby raised a finger. "What about curiosity?"

"That," Zara said, "is your greatest weapon."

Mia glanced at me. "And your biggest risk."

I nodded. She was right.

Because caring made you sloppy. Made you rush. Made you reveal too much too soon.

"Here's the thing," Zara said, softer now. "None of us wants to be wrong."

She looked around the group.

"If we accuse the wrong person, even silently, we break trust. And trust is the one thing we can't afford to lose."

Madison shifted her weight. "What if we find something scary?"

Zara's gaze softened when it landed on her. "Then we tell each other. Immediately."

"And not grown-ups?" Madison asked.

Zara hesitated.

"Eventually," she said. "But not until we understand what we're seeing."

That answer sat heavy in the air.

I realised then how strange it was that we were doing this at all. A group of kids standing around a park table, dividing up adults like puzzle pieces, talking about systems and leverage and access points.

And yet... it made sense.

Because no one else was looking the way we were.

I cleared my throat. "So… after we test them?"

Zara nodded. "We regroup. Compare patterns. Look for inconsistencies."

"And if someone reacts badly?" I asked.

"Badly how?" she asked.

"Too defensive," I said. "Too calm. Too interested."

Zara smiled faintly. "Then we narrow again."

Sam grinned. "Like a funnel."

"Like a funnel," Zara agreed.

Toby looked thoughtful. "Funnels get smaller."

"Yes," Zara said. "That's the point."

We stood there for a moment after that, no one rushing to leave.

The wind moved through the trees. Somewhere, a dog barked. The park kept being a park.

But underneath it all, the lines had been drawn.

Roles assigned.

Boundaries set.

I felt the weight of Mrs Calder's name settle into my chest; my teacher, my test.

Mia caught my eye and gave a small nod, like she was saying, *we've got this* even if she didn't know how yet.

Sam bumped my shoulder. "Hey."

"What?"

"Being kids," he said. "We're great at that. It is what we do best."

I smiled despite myself.

He was right.

And for the first time since this all started, I felt something close to steady.

Not safe.

But ready.

CHAPTER 19

Mrs Calder

We divided the suspects the way adults divide chores—carefully, with logic, and pretending feelings weren't involved.

Which, of course, meant feelings were *absolutely* involved.

The park table was chipped and covered in old scratches, initials carved into the wood by kids who'd come before us and thought their names needed to last forever. Zara stood at the head of it like she owned the place, notebook open, pencil hovering just above the page as if the wrong movement might set something off.

She had written nothing yet.

That was how I knew this part mattered.

"Okay," she said. "We don't rush this."

Sam immediately rocked back on his heels. "I hate sentences that start like that."

Zara ignored him.

She scanned our faces one by one, as if she were measuring a weight we didn't know we were carrying. Mia sat straighter than usual. Chloe hugged her sketchbook to her chest. Maya watched quietly, eyes flicking between Zara's pencil and the page. Madison lingered just behind Mia, hands clasped, trying to take up as little space as possible. Toby stood beside Sam, helmet under one arm as if he'd removed it out of respect.

Then Zara looked at me.

"Mrs Calder," she said.

Just my teacher's name.

Nothing else.

My stomach dipped so fast it felt like I'd missed a step on the stairs.

"I get my teacher," I said.

It came out flatter than I meant it to, like I'd already accepted it even though I hadn't. Mrs Calder. The person who handed back my tests. The person who knew my handwriting. The person who could tell when I wasn't listening, even when I pretended, I was.

"Yes," Zara replied calmly. "You're already inside her orbit. That gives you cover."

I nodded, even though the word *orbit* made me feel like I was about to be flung into space without a helmet.

"And trauma," Sam added helpfully.

I shot him a look. "You are not helping."

"I'm adding realism," he said.

Zara didn't even sigh this time. She just made a small mark next to my name in her notebook, like she'd mentally ticked a box labelled *Leo: emotionally compromised but useful.*

"Mia," Zara said, shifting her gaze.

Mia straightened immediately, as if she were responding to a call only, she could hear.

"Mrs Henley is mine," Mia said before Zara could finish.

Her voice was steady, but I saw the way her shoulders squared, the way she inhaled as if she was bracing herself. Mrs Henley—the office, the forms, the paper trail that touched everything.

Zara studied her for a second. "You're sure?"

Mia nodded. "I can do it."

There was something fierce in her eyes then, something quiet but solid. I felt that familiar warmth in my chest and pushed it down. This wasn't the time.

Zara nodded. "Alright. Librarian for me."

She wrote *Mrs Dalloway* in neat, controlled letters.

"That tracks," Jasmine murmured. "She sees *everything*."

"And no one ever notices her noticing," Maya added.

Zara didn't comment. She just underlined the name once.

Then, Sam and Toby raised their hands together.

Perfectly in sync.

"Mr Bell," they said in unison.

Zara closed her eyes.

Not dramatically. Not annoyed.

Briefly. Like someone counting to three.

"This," she said carefully, opening them again, "is why I didn't want to assign him to you."

Sam beamed. "We're uniquely qualified."

"At annoying adults," Toby added earnestly.

"Exactly," Sam said, nodding as if this was a badge of honour.

Zara pressed her lips together. "You realise this is a *serious* investigation."

"Yes," Sam said. "And we take annoyance very seriously."

Toby nodded. "We specialise."

Zara exhaled through her nose. "Fine. But if you get detention—"

"We won't," Sam said quickly.

"If you *almost* get detention—"

"We'll retreat," Toby promised.

"If you provoke him—"

Sam held up a finger. "Define provoke."

Zara stared at him.

He lowered his hand.

"Okay," she said. "Assignments stand."

She tapped the notebook shut.

"And now we repeat the rules," she said. "Because someone always forgets."

Sam opened his mouth.

Zara raised an eyebrow.

He closed it again.

"No accusations," she said. "Not even implied ones."

"No confrontations," Mia added.

"Write nothing down where it could be found," Zara continued.

"No notes, no lists, no doodles that accidentally look like maps."

Sam glanced at the dirt near his shoes where he'd already drawn something suspiciously diagram-like and scuffed it out with his foot.

"And most importantly," Zara said, voice lowering slightly, "no acting like detectives."

That one hit harder than the rest.

I felt it in my chest.

Because we *felt* like detectives.

Like we were solving something important. Like we were smarter than the adults who hadn't noticed—or hadn't acted.

But that was the trap.

"We're just kids," Zara reminded us. "Being a kid is the disguise. It should be what we do best."

I thought about that.

About how being a kid meant asking questions that didn't sound dangerous. Being in places without raising alarms. Being ignored when you wanted to be heard and when you didn't expect it.

That part was easy, and the hard part was pretending not to care.

Sam rocked forward again. "What does 'being a kid' actually look like?"

Zara considered. "It looks like homework questions. Lost items. Bathroom passes. Casual conversations."

"Annoying conversations," Sam clarified.

"Yes," Zara said. "Especially those."

Toby raised a finger. "What about curiosity?"

"That," Zara said, "is your greatest weapon."

Mia glanced at me. "And your biggest risk."

I nodded. She was right.

Because caring made you sloppy. Made you rush. Made you reveal too much, too soon.

"Here's the thing," Zara said, softer now. "None of us wants to be wrong."

She looked around the group.

"If we accuse the wrong person, even silently, we break trust. And trust is the one thing we can't afford to lose."

Madison shifted her weight. "What if we find something scary?"

Zara's gaze softened when it landed on her. "Then we tell each other. Immediately."

"And not grown-ups?" Madison asked.

Zara hesitated.

"Eventually," she said. "But not until we understand what we're seeing."

That answer hung heavy in the air.

I realised then how strange it was that we were doing this at all. A group of kids standing around a park table, dividing up adults like puzzle pieces, talking about systems and leverage and access points.

And yet... it made sense.

Because no one else was looking the way we were.

I cleared my throat. "So... after we test them?"

Zara nodded. "We regroup. Compare patterns. Look for inconsistencies."

"And if someone reacts badly?" I asked.

"Badly how?" she asked.

"Too defensive," I said. "Too calm. Too interested."

Zara smiled faintly. "Then we narrow again."

Sam grinned. "Like a funnel."

"Like a funnel," Zara agreed.

Toby looked thoughtful. "Funnels get smaller."

"Yes," Zara said. "That's the point."

We stood there for a moment after that, no one rushing to leave.

The wind moved through the trees. Somewhere, a dog barked. The park kept being a park.

But underneath it all, the lines had been drawn.

Roles assigned.

Boundaries set.

I felt the weight of Mrs Calder's name settle into my chest; my teacher, my test.

Mia caught my eye and gave a small nod, as if she was saying, *we've got this* even if she didn't know how yet.

Sam bumped my shoulder. "Hey."

"What?"

"Being kids," he said. "We're great at that. It is what we do best."

I smiled despite myself.

He was right.

And for the first time since this all started, I felt something close to steady.

Not safe.

But ready.

CHAPTER 20

Mrs Dalloway

Zara

If there's one thing I've learned about secrets, it's that they don't hide in loud places. They hide where silence is normal. They hide where people lower their voices without thinking, where footsteps soften, where even breathing feels like it should be polite.

They hide in libraries.

Mrs Dalloway's domain is a long, rectangular room that smells like old paper and glue and the faintest hint of dust—like the air itself is preserving something. The moment you step inside, the school changes. The buzzing corridors vanish. The shouting oval disappears. The building becomes gentle and careful.

Which means it is also a perfect place for something not gentle.

I arrived at lunchtime on Tuesday, three minutes early, because being early is a kind of control, and I don't apologise for it. I chose a seat with clear sightlines: the front corner near the windows, angled so I could see the circulation desk, the shelves, and the entrance.

I opened a book I had no intention of reading, then I waited.

Mrs Dalloway stood behind the desk, sorting returns. She moved with calm efficiency—stamping, scanning, sliding books into neat stacks. Her hair was greying at the temples, pulled into a bun that never shifted. Her cardigan sleeves were rolled to the same point on both arms. Everything about her was symmetrical, contained, measured.

I've learned to distrust measured. Measured can be calm, yes, but it can also be rehearsed.

A group of Year Twos wandered in first, guided by a teacher who looked tired in the way adults do when they've stopped expecting quiet to exist. The children scattered to the picture book area like marbles released onto the floor.

Mrs Dalloway greeted them with the same soft voice she used for everyone.

"Hello, darlings. Inside voices."

Inside voices.

The phrase has always bothered me.

Not because it's wrong, but because it teaches you something without telling you: that there are voices meant for inside, and voices meant to stay hidden.

I watched her hands.

Hands tell you what mouths won't.

Mrs Dalloway's fingers didn't shake.

Her movements weren't hurried. She didn't glance at the door too often or press her lips together after speaking. The calm didn't feel like a performance, but performances are exactly what I'm trained to look for.

I pretended to read, but I didn't I listened.

The trick with testing someone like Mrs Dalloway is that you can't ask directly. Direct questions bounce off her like pebbles. She's built to handle direct. She has procedures, policies, signs on the wall. *No food. No running. Ask at the desk.* Direct questions are her favourite kind. She can answer them feeling nothing.

So, I needed a question that slid under the policy layer.

A trick question within a question, like Leo had done with Mrs Calder.

Only Leo's trick had been emotional.

Mine would be structural.

At exactly twelve twenty, I stood up and walked to the desk with three books in my hands. Not random books. Books that mattered.

A Year Five biography of a local politician, or a thick history book with a plain cover, and a children's mystery novel with a dog on the front.

The mystery book was the key, while the others were camouflage.

Mrs Dalloway looked up and smiled. "Hello, Zara."

She knows my name.

Librarians always do. They know the names of the children who return books on time. It's like a reward system.

"Hi," I said lightly. "I'm returning these."

She scanned them, stamped them, placed them in a stack.

"Any new recommendations?" I asked, as if this was a normal conversation.

She brightened slightly. "We have a new shipment in. Some excellent junior mysteries."

"Mysteries," I repeated. "That's actually why I'm here."

She tilted her head. "Oh?"

I tapped the dog-covered book. "I found this in the wrong section yesterday. It was shelved in history."

Mrs Dalloway blinked once. "Was it?"

"Yes," I said. "It seemed... misplaced."

Misplaced was a safe word.

Misplaced doesn't accuse.

Misplaced invites correction.

Her smile didn't move.

"That happens," she said. "Children put books back wherever they like."

"Right," I said, nodding. "But the weird part was that it had a note inside."

There it was.

The first hook.

Mrs Dalloway's scanning hand paused.

Not in mid-air. Not dramatic. Just a pause long enough to be real. Her eyes flicked down to the book cover, then back up to me.

"What sort of note?" she asked.

This was when many adults gave advice. They tell you not to touch it, not to read it, to bring it to the office. If she were innocent and purely procedural, she'd tell me what to do next. If she were guilty, she'd try to control what I'd seen.

I offered a third option—a lie that sounded true.

"Like a little reminder," I said. "Not scary. Just strange. It said something about 'watching.'"

Her eyes narrowed slightly, the first expression that wasn't a standard library face.

"Watching," she repeated.

Her voice was still soft, but there was weight behind it now, like a book dropped onto a table.

I kept my face neutral.

"Yeah. It made me wonder if people leave notes in books a lot."

She held my gaze.

Then she did something unexpected. She didn't ask for the book, she didn't demand to see the note, she didn't launch into procedure she just lowered her voice.

"Children leave all sorts of things in books," she said. "Bookmarks. Drawings. Notes meant for friends."

"Do adults?" I asked as casually as I could manage.

Mrs Dalloway's smile returned, but it had changed. Less warm. More careful.

"Adults," she said, "should know better."

That sentence could mean everything or nothing.

I leaned slightly closer. "So, if an adult did, you'd notice."

"Yes," she said without hesitation.

"I notice what comes across my desk."

Interesting.

Not *I notice what happens in the library.* Not *I notice children's behaviour.* Specifically, what comes across my desk.

Paper flow and control points.

"What about things that don't come across your desk?" I asked.

It was too direct, and I felt it the moment it left my mouth.

Mrs Dalloway's expression hardened, not angry, but closed.

"I'm not sure what you're implying," she said.

There. The wall. I stepped back mentally, adjusted.

"I'm not implying anything," I said quickly.

"I just worry about people getting into trouble for silly things."

That's my second hook: guilt.

Not hers, someone else's.

Mrs Dalloway studied me again.

Behind her, the Year Two teacher was trying to coax a child away from the computers. The kid was whining loudly enough that it made a small bubble of chaos.

Mrs Dalloway didn't look away from me.

"You're a serious child," she said quietly.

"I'm just observant," I replied.

She nodded once.

"Observant children often carry burdens they didn't ask for."

My stomach tightened.

That sounded too accurate, too darn sharp.

"Do you think something's going on?" I asked.

Mrs Dalloway inhaled slowly, as if she were tasting the air before speaking.

Then she said, "I think children have always passed messages in schools."

Not an answer.

A truth dressed as a dodge.

"And adults?" I pressed softer now.

Her gaze flicked to the entrance, to the hallway, to the world outside her quiet rectangle, and then back to me.

"Adults," she said, "often pretend they don't see what they see."

That was the closest thing to a confession I'd ever heard from someone who hadn't confessed.

I felt something shift in my mind.

She wasn't the inside person. Not in the way we meant.

She wasn't delivering notes. But she knew the *ecosystem* of messages. She knew how information moved.

Which meant she could see patterns and choose what to ignore.

"Mrs Dalloway," I said carefully, "if someone was being hurt by messages, if it wasn't harmless, would you intervene?"

Her eyes softened for the first time.

"Yes," she said immediately. "But only if I knew who was holding the knife."

Knife, not a pen, not paper, but a knife.

That word chilled me.

"You think it's dangerous," I said.

"I think," she replied, "that children's fear is never harmless."

I nodded slowly, and then I did the ultimate test.

I picked up the mystery book again, flipped it open, and pretended to find the imaginary note.

"Oh," I said lightly. "Here it is."

Mrs Dalloway didn't reach for it. She didn't lean in. She didn't flinch. She watched only my face, not the page.

That told me everything.

People who want control grab the object, and people who want truth watch the person.

"Thank you," I said, closing the book.

She nodded. "Zara."

"Yes?"

"If you're carrying something too heavy," she said softly, "you don't have to carry it alone."

I held her gaze.

For one second, I considered telling her everything.

Then I remembered Leo's story about the woman on the path and her smile. The possibility of an inside person. The risk of trusting the wrong adult.

So, I did what I always do.

I nodded. "I know."

And I walked away, heartbeat steady but mind racing.

Outside, the school noise crashed back into me—shouting, running, the scrape of shoes on concrete. Life resumed its normal pace as if nothing important had happened in the quiet rectangle.

But something had happened.

Mrs Dalloway wasn't our inside person.

She didn't smell like control; she smelled like awareness and restraint.

Which meant she could become an ally, or she could become a blind spot we'd underestimated.

When I met the group after school, I gave them the facts.

"She noticed," I told them. "She didn't panic. She didn't demand anything. She watched *me*, not the note."

Leo's face tightened with concentration. Mia hugged her arms, thinking.

Sam frowned. "So, she's... not an evil librarian?"

"No," I said. "She's not delivering notes."

Toby tilted his head. "But she might know who is."

"Exactly," I said.

And as we stood there, the sun lowering behind the trees, I realised something that made my skin prickle.

If Mrs Dalloway had noticed the ecosystem, then the inside person wasn't someone clumsy.

They were someone careful, someone who knew where the blind spots were, someone who moved through systems as if they belonged there, someone who didn't just place notes, someone who understood silence, just like a library.

CHAPTER 21

Mrs Henley

Mia

The office smells like paper, disinfectant, and secrets. I know that sounds dramatic, but once you pay attention, everything smells like secrets. Especially places where adults decide things without telling kids why.

Mrs Henley sits behind the front desk with her cardigan sleeves pushed up and a pen tucked neatly behind her ear. She smiles the way people do when they want you to feel safe quickly. It's a friendly smile. Warm. Familiar. The kind that says *I've got this* even when you don't know what *this* is.

That's why Zara assigned her to me.

"Because you don't scare easily and you listen when people talk around the thing they don't want to say." Zara had said.

I hadn't known whether that was a compliment or a jab.

Now, standing just outside the office with a hall pass in my hand, I wasn't sure I wanted it to be true, so I took a breath and stepped inside.

"Hi, Mrs Henley," I said.

She looked up immediately, a smile already in place. "Hello, Mia. What can I do for you?"

I held up the pass.

"Mrs Calder sent me to drop this off. And she said to ask about the lost property form."

"That sounds like her," Mrs Henley said, reaching for the paper. Her fingers were quick. Efficient. Used to handling things that moved through many hands.

She glanced at the pass, nodded, then turned to a tray beside her. Papers, forms, notes to parents, slips with names and dates, and, my goodness, so much paper.

"Lost property," she said. "Is it clothing or lunch items?"

"Both?" I said, letting uncertainty wobble my voice just enough to sound real.

She chuckled. "That happens."

She slid a form toward me and began explaining how to fill it out, tapping each section with her pen. I watched her hands. Watched how she paused, only briefly, when a teacher walked past the doorway. Watched how she lowered her voice when a parent came in, then raised it again when they left.

She controlled the flow of information like traffic.

"That goes here," she said. "And if you don't know the date, just write 'approximate.'"

Approximate.

I nodded. "Okay. Thanks."

I didn't leave.

Mrs Henley looked up again, curious but not irritated. "Was there anything else?"

This was the moment. Leo had called it a "trick question within a question." Zara called it "behavioural prompting." I called it terrifying.

"I was wondering," I said, "how notes get delivered to classrooms."

Her pen paused for just for a second, but I saw it.

"Well," she said smoothly, "teachers usually collect their own messages. Sometimes the office delivers them if it's urgent."

"Oh," I said. "So, like, if a note wasn't official?"

She smiled again, a little tighter this time.

"We don't deliver unofficial notes."

"Right," I said quickly. "I just meant, like, sometimes notes appear in places. Like reminders or messages."

Her eyes sharpened, not angry, but as if assessing.

"Why do you ask?" she said gently.

Because I'm terrified, or because someone is watching my friends, or because a woman smiled at my school like it was hers?

Instead, I shrugged.

"It just seems like a lot of paper moves through here."

That was true, which was a lot safer than a lie.

Mrs Henley leaned back slightly.

"Paper moves through here," she said. "But only what's meant to."

Only what's meant to.

I filled out the lost property form while she watched me. Not closely, but casually, maybe too casually.

When I finished, she took it and slipped it into a folder without checking the details.

"Anything else, Mia?" she asked.

I hesitated and then took a risk.

"Do you ever worry," I said softly, "that things end up in the wrong hands?"

Her smile didn't falter.

"No," she said. "That's why there are systems."

Systems.

The word landed heavily.

"And if something *did*?" I pressed.

She met my eyes fully now.

"Then someone would notice."

I nodded; I thanked her and left.

In the hallway, my legs felt shaky.

Not because I'd found proof, but because I hadn't.

Mrs Henley hadn't slipped, she hadn't over-corrected; she hadn't seized control or deflected too hard, but she hadn't opened up either.

She'd stayed contained.

At lunch, I found Leo near the garden beds. He looked up immediately, reading my face the way he always did now.

"Well?" he asked quietly.

"I don't know," I said. "She's careful."

Zara joined us moments later. "Careful how?"

"Like she knows where every piece of paper should be," I said. "And doesn't like imagining it anywhere else."

Zara nodded slowly. "Did she break routine?"

"No," I said. "She reinforced it."

"That can mean two things," Zara said. "Either she's exactly what she appears to be, or she's very good at not appearing."

Leo exhaled. "So, not cleared."

"No," Zara said. "But not confirmed."

As the bell rang, I glanced back toward the office.

Mrs Henley was laughing with a parent now, pen tucked behind her ear, cardigan sleeves still rolled up.

Perfectly normal, and that's what scared me.

Because the Watcher loved systems, and Mrs Henley *was* one.

Still, as I walked away, one thought settled in my chest, heavy but steady: if she was the inside person, she hadn't expected *me*.

And if she wasn't?

Then she was closer to the Watcher than she realised.

Either way, the office was no longer neutral ground.

And next time, I wouldn't walk in alone.

CHAPTER 22

Mr Bell

Sam

People underestimate how powerful it is to be annoying. They think annoying is accidental, or rude, or something you get told off for, but annoying, *strategic* annoying, is a tool.

That's why Zara assigned Mr Bell to us.

"Well," she'd said, rubbing her forehead, "if anyone can make an adult break pattern without realising it, it's you two."

I'd taken that as praise while Toby saluted.

So that afternoon, Toby and I positioned ourselves exactly where Mr Bell didn't want us to be: near the maintenance shed, beside the trolleys, close enough that he couldn't ignore us but far enough that telling us to move would require effort.

Mr Bell was sweeping.

He always swept as if he were punishing the ground for existing.

Back and forth. Sharp strokes. Angry bristles.

I nudged Toby. "Phase one."

Toby nodded solemnly, and we wandered over.

"Hi Mr Bell," I said cheerfully.

He didn't look up. "You boys should head home."

"We are," Toby said. "Slowly."

Mr Bell sighed. Loudly.

Good. First crack.

I leaned closer to the trolley. "Is that a new broom?"

"No," he said.

"Because it looks like a newer model," I continued. "The bristles are angled differently."

Toby squinted. "Yeah. That's a 35-degree angle. Older brooms were 40."

Mr Bell stopped sweeping just for a second, then he resumed.

"Go home," he muttered.

Toby stepped closer. "Do you keep records of your equipment?"

Mr Bell's sweeping slowed.

"Why would I?" he snapped.

"Oh," Toby said innocently. "Because my uncle keeps records of his tools. He says it helps track wear patterns."

"I don't need help to track my tools," Mr Bell said sharply.

I nodded sympathetically. "Of course not. You seem very organised."

That did it.

He stopped sweeping completely and turned to face us.

"What do you want?" he demanded.

Phase two.

"Nothing," I said quickly.

"We were just wondering how long you've worked here," Toby added.

Mr Bell frowned. "That's none of your business."

"Long time?" I guessed.

"Long enough," he said.

"Longer than Mrs Calder?" Toby asked.

"No."

"Mrs Dalloway?" I tried.

He hesitated.

"Maybe."

Toby and I exchanged a look.

I smiled brightly. "So, you've seen a lot of changes."

Mr Bell's jaw tightened.

"You boys ask too many questions."

"That's what they say about scientists," Toby replied.

"I'm not a scientist," Mr Bell snapped.

"No," I agreed. "You're more behind-the-scenes."

That was when it happened. He glanced toward the shed door, just a glance, too quick, too reflexive, and I pretended not to notice.

Toby didn't; Toby never missed a reflex.

Toby

Mr Bell's eyes moved before his mouth did, and that, I think, is important because people who are hiding something check exits, or objects, or places where something is stored. It's instinct.

My dad does it when he forgets where he parked the car.

The shed.

I filed that away and then I crouched suddenly.

Mr Bell jumped.

"What are you doing now?" he barked.

"Ant," I said.

"There's no ant."

"There was," I replied. "It moved."

Mr Bell's face twitched.

Sam leaned against the trolley casually.

"You must get a lot of ants in here."

"No."

"Rodents?" I asked.

"No."

"Paper?" Sam added.

Mr Bell's grip tightened on the broom.

"Paper doesn't crawl," he said.

"But it *moves*," Sam said.

I nodded. "Especially when people put it in places."

Silence, not angry silence but measured silence.

Mr Bell straightened. "You two need to leave. Now."

Phase three.

Compliance, but not retreat.

"Okay," Sam said easily. "One last thing."

Mr Bell closed his eyes briefly.

"Yes?"

"Do you ever," Sam said, "deliver messages for other people?"

Mr Bell opened his eyes.

"No," he said firmly. "That's not my job."

"Even if they asked?" I pressed.

"Especially then."

His answer was fast — way too fast.

Sam tilted his head. "What if they didn't ask?"

Mr Bell stared at us.

"You're playing games," he said.

"Yes," Sam agreed. "But not the kind you think."

That's when Mr Bell did something interesting.

He laughed, not a genuine laugh, but it was maybe like a release.

"You kids think you're very clever," he said. "You think you've figured something out."

Sam shrugged. "Sometimes."

Mr Bell leaned closer, lowering his voice.

"Let me give you some advice."

I leaned in too.

"Stay out of grown-up business," he said. "It doesn't end well."

That wasn't a denial; that wasn't even anger, but that was a warning, and I felt a chill, but Sam didn't.

He grinned. "Thanks. We love advice."

Mr Bell straightened, clearly done. "Go. Home."

We went, but slowly.

Sam

We didn't speak until we were well away from the shed.

Then Toby stopped walking.

"He's not the inside person," Toby said.

I blinked. "What?"

"He's something," Toby continued, "but not the *inside person*."

I frowned. "He didn't deny knowing things."

"Yes," Toby said. "But he didn't enjoy it."

I thought about that.

Mr Bell liked power that showed; he liked feeling important and enjoyed being noticed.

The inside person liked control that stayed invisible.

Mr Bell cracked too easily.

"He's being used," I said slowly.

Toby nodded. "Or threatened."

I shuddered. "I don't like that."

"Me neither."

We regrouped with Leo, Mia, and Zara after school.

Zara listened carefully as we reported everything—every glance, every pause, every warning.

When we finished, she nodded once.

"Mr Bell isn't the inside person," she said. "But he knows something."

Leo's jaw tightened. "Which means the Watcher has leverage."

Mia hugged her arms. "That's worse."

I looked back toward the shed.

"He was scared," I said quietly.

Zara met my eyes. "So am I."

And for the first time since this all began, I realised something else.

The Watcher didn't just watch.

She pressed people, systems, and on weaknesses.

And the real danger wasn't the one who smiled at the school from the path.

It was the one inside, still invisible, still untouched, still calm.

And we hadn't met them yet.

CHAPTER 23

Regroup and a New Strategy

We met behind the gym again. Not because it was a secret place—everyone knew kids stood back there—but because it was overlooked in the way unimportant things often are. The bins smelled, and the concrete was cracked. Teachers rarely wandered past unless they were specifically looking for someone.

Which, Zara said, made it perfect.

By now, regrouping had become a ritual.

We stood in a loose circle, backpacks at our feet, bodies angled inward as if we were trying to protect something fragile in the middle. Chloe leaned against the wall; sketchbook tucked under her arm. Maya sat cross-legged on the ground, hands folded. Jasmine paced, dramatic even when she was trying not to be. Madison hovered close to Mia, eyes wide, absorbing everything. Sam and Toby stood shoulder to shoulder, unusually quiet.

I cleared my throat.

"So," I said. "We've tested them."

Zara nodded. "All four."

Mia exhaled slowly. "And none of them fit."

That was the problem.

Mrs Calder—out. Mr Bell—not inside, though definitely tangled. Mrs Henley—careful, but contained, and Mrs Dalloway—aware, restrained, watching the system rather than controlling it.

Four adults and four no suspects.

Zero answers.

Zara flipped through her notebook, pages full of arrows, symbols, and notes that only made sense if you'd been there for every conversation.

"Logic," she said, tapping the page, "leads us somewhere uncomfortable."

Sam frowned. "I don't like uncomfortable logic."

"No one does," Zara replied. "But it's usually right."

Mia looked at me. "Say it."

I hesitated and then said it.

"It has to be a student."

The words sat there between us.

Not dramatic, not explosive, just heavy.

"A student," Jasmine repeated. "Our age?"

"Or close," Zara said. "Someone who can move freely. Someone who understands lockers, transitions, blind spots."

"And" Maya added quietly, "someone who blends."

I felt a chill.

Because blending wasn't about being invisible.

It was about being *forgettable*.

"Why would a student do it?" Madison asked softly.

No one answered straight away.

Sam shifted his weight. Toby stared at the ground.

Finally, Zara spoke. "Because students have the best leverage on other students."

Fear landed differently when it came from someone your own age. It stuck. It echoed.

"And" Mia said slowly, "because a student could be watched without realising, they were being used."

That thought made my stomach churn.

"A go-between," I said. "The Watcher outside. A student inside."

Zara nodded. "A courier."

"Or a collaborator," Jasmine said.

"Or someone who thinks they're special," Sam muttered.

Everyone looked at him.

"What?" he said defensively. "Some people like feeling chosen."

That was uncomfortably accurate.

Zara closed her notebook.

"We don't accuse. We observe."

"So how do we narrow it down?" I asked.

Zara's eyes flicked toward the oval, where kids from our year were already running, shouting, spilling into recess like marbles.

"We'll increase the sample size," she said.

Mia frowned. "You mean watch more people?"

"Yes," Zara replied. "All of them."

I blinked. "All of Year Five?"

"During recess," Zara clarified. "Movement patterns. Group changes. Who watches whom?"

Sam's eyes widened. "That's a lot of people."

"Yes," Zara said. "Which means we need cover."

"And numbers," Mia added.

Jasmine smiled. "I can handle numbers."

"So can I," Chloe said softly.

Madison nodded eagerly. "I'll watch from the benches."

Maya folded her hands. "I'll track routines."

I looked at Sam and Toby. "You two?"

Sam hesitated. "We're sworn to secrecy."

"Yes," Zara said. "Which means you observe, not talk."

Sam nodded.

"That's fine," he said. "I can do that."

I should have known then.

The next day, recess arrived like a ticking clock.

The plan was simple—again, dangerously simple.

Everyone spread out.

No obvious clustering, no whispering, just watching.

I stood near the bubblers, pretending to wait my turn. Mia sat on the low wall, swinging her legs. Zara leaned against the library doors. Jasmine drifted between groups like a social butterfly with a mission.

Sam and Toby were near the climbing frame.

That's where things went wrong.

At first, Sam did exactly what he was supposed to do.

He watched, he counted, he noticed who moved between groups and who stayed fixed; he noticed who looked toward the lockers even during recess.

Who hovered near teachers without reason?

He notices too much, and when Sam notices too much, he fidgets.

Toby noticed *that*.

"You're twitching," Toby whispered.

"I'm thinking," Sam whispered back.

"You think loudly."

Sam shoved his hands into his pockets. "Everyone's moving weird."

"That's because you're watching them," Toby said reasonably.

Sam swallowed. "What if they notice?"

"That's the point," Toby said. "To see who notices back."

Unfortunately, Sam's friend group had noticed something else.

"Why's your brother staring at us?" Ben asked, pointing subtly in my direction.

Sam froze.

"What?" he said.

"Leo," another kid said. "He keeps looking over here."

Sam's heart started pounding. He could feel it in his ears. In his hands. In the space between thoughts.

This was bad; this was terrible.

"Why would Leo stare at us?" Ben pressed.

Toby tugged Sam's sleeve. "Ignore it."

But ignoring things had never been Sam's strength.

"Well—" Sam began.

He stopped and started again.

"Well, it's because—"

Toby's eyes widened. "Sam—"

"—there's this Watcher," Sam blurted.

The world seemed to spin wildly.

Toby stared at him in horror.

Ben frowned. "A what?"

"A Watcher," Sam said, words spilling out now, unstoppable. "A woman who watches the school from the path and leaves notes and might have an inside person, and we're trying to figure out who it is and—"

"SAM," Toby hissed.

Too late.

Three more kids leaned in.

"Notes?" someone asked.

"What an inside person?" another whispered.

Sam's brain screamed, *stop*.

His mouth ignored it.

"They're anonymous," Sam continued, panicking. "Different colours. Pink, yellow, and blue, and one white one, and Leo found the first one and..."

Toby covered his face with his hands.

Across the oval, I felt it before I saw it.

That shift, the buzz, heads turning and whispers spreading.

Mia stiffened against the wall.

Zara's eyes snapped toward the climbing frame.

Sam finally realised what he'd done.

His voice trailed off.

"...and we weren't supposed to tell anyone."

Silence.

Then—

"That's not funny," Ben said.

"I'm not joking," Sam whispered.

Someone laughed nervously. "You're messing with us."

Sam shook his head. "I swear."

Toby grabbed his arm. "We need to go. Now."

But the damage was already been done.

The story didn't stop with Sam's group.

Stories never do.

By the time the bell rang, half of Year Five knew *something*.

Not the truth, but enough, enough to ask questions, enough to look differently, enough to notice Leo Marshall watching.

Behind the gym after school, the regrouping was not calm.

"What did you do?" Zara demanded.

Sam stood still, face pale. "I panicked."

"You told them?" Mia asked, disbelief creeping into her voice.

Sam nodded once. "I told them everything."

Not anger, not shouting, just the sound of our plans collapsing in people's heads.

Zara closed her eyes.

I stepped forward. "Sam—"

"I'm sorry," he blurted. "I didn't mean to. They asked and I—"

"I know," I said softly.

Because I did. Sam didn't like secrets. They pressed on him. Made him feel as if he had been holding his breath for too long.

Zara opened her eyes again.

"Well," she said, voice tight, "the strategy has changed."

"How?" Jasmine asked.

Zara looked toward the oval, now empty.

"Because now," she said, "the Watcher knows we're close."

"And" Mia added, "the inside person knows we're watching students."

Sam swallowed hard. "I messed up."

"Yes," Zara said. "You did."

Sam flinched.

"But" Zara continued, "mistakes create ripples."

She looked at me. "And ripples show patterns."

I frowned. "You think Sam did us a favour?"

"Not intentionally," Zara said. "But yes."

"How?" Sam asked weakly.

"Because" Zara replied, "whoever the inside person is... will react."

I thought about that.

The three things we always discuss: fear, control, and silence.

If the inside person was a student, and they'd just learned the net was widening—

"They'll change behaviour," I said.

"Exactly," Zara said. "And that's what we watch next."

Sam let out a shaky breath. "So, I'm not fired?"

"No," Zara said. "But you're on observation duty only."

Toby nodded solemnly. "I'll supervise him."

Sam managed a small smile.

As we packed up, I felt something strange settle in my chest.

The plan hadn't broken. It just had bent.

And sometimes, bending showed you exactly where the pressure was coming from.

Sam had made an error, a big one, but in doing so, he'd shaken the board.

And now, somewhere in Year Five, someone was deciding what to do next. Which meant we were closer than ever.

CHAPTER 24

The Cost of Secrecy

The secret didn't explode. It slid, it seeped, and it *spread*.

By Monday morning, the school felt different in a way that was impossible to point at and impossible to ignore—like when the air goes heavy before rain and everyone pretends; they don't notice until the first drop hits someone on the head.

People were looking at me, not really staring, not obviously but just... checking.

Checking my locker as they walked past, checking my face when I laughed, checking to see if I was checking them back.

I hated it.

I reached locker 217 and already knew something was wrong before I opened it.

The door resisted for half a second—heavier than usual.

That should've been my first clue.

When it finally swung open, papers spilled out.

Not fluttered but *spilled*.

Pink.

Yellow.

Blue.

White.

Orange.

Purple, yes, actual purple this time.

Lined paper ripped from notebooks.

Printer paper.

Cardstock.

Some were folded carefully, others crumpled aggressively, and one with a doodle of a stick figure waving.

They slid over my shoes, onto the floor, and against the lockers on either side.

For a second, I just stood there with my brain refusing to process the amount.

Then Sam appeared beside me.

He took one look.

"Oh," he said softly. "Oh, no."

More kids slowed as they passed.

Someone laughed, someone whistled, and someone said, "Bro, you're popular now."

I dropped to my knees and started scooping them up—not to read, just to get them *away*.

My hands moved faster than my thoughts.

Mia appeared on my other side, eyes wide.

"This is a lot," she said.

"That's one word for it," Zara said from behind us.

She crouched too, scanning the notes without touching them, her face tight.

"This is contamination," she muttered.

"Contamination?" Sam echoed.

"Noise," Zara said. "Too much noise."

The bell rang, and no one moved.

A teacher shouted from down the hall, "In class, everyone!"

The crowd thinned reluctantly, and I shoved the notes into my bag until it bulged like it was about to confess something.

In class, I didn't learn anything. I kept feeling the weight of the bag against my leg, like it was breathing, and at recess, it got worse.

Someone slipped a note into my hand as I passed the bubblers; another landed on my desk when I wasn't looking, then a folded square appeared on my chair.

I stopped counting at thirty-seven.

By lunchtime, the bench near the garden beds was covered.

We spread them out carefully, like evidence and like landmines.

Some were stupid.

Are you famous now?

My cousin says you're a spy lol

Blink twice if the Watcher is real

Some were funny.

Dear Leo, I too enjoy lockers.

I am yours sincerely, Anonymous.

If you're watching me, I will watch you watching me and see how you like it.

Some were not.

You should stop before you get hurt.

People who look too much miss what's behind them.

You don't know who you're protecting.

Mia read one and flinched.

Sam picked up another and immediately put it back down like it burned.

"This is chaos," Jasmine said. "Unorganised, dramatic chaos."

"The Watcher must be loving this," Zara said flatly.

That felt true.

Whoever she was, outside, smiling at the school, this was her perfect weather.

Fear mixed with humour and truth buried under jokes with signals drowned in noise for confusion is camouflage.

I rubbed my face with both hands.

"I can't tell what matters anymore," I said. "It's all just—everything."

"That's the cost of secrecy breaking," Zara replied.

"Once it's public, control shifts."

"To whom?" I asked.

Zara didn't answer.

Maya spoke instead.

"To whoever can hide in the crowd."

That made my stomach sink.

We were so busy trying to see everyone that we'd forgotten what crowds did.

They erased edges.

Toby had been quiet. Uncharacteristically quiet.

He knelt at the far end of the bench, sorting notes by something only he could see—maybe size, maybe fold, maybe weight. His helmet sat beside him on the ground, which meant he was thinking hard enough to need extra oxygen.

He picked up a note I hadn't noticed before.

Green. Not pale green. Not mint. Deep leaf green, almost emerald.

It was folded differently too—sharp creases, precise, no doodles, and no smudges.

Toby held it between his fingers as if it might move.

His eyes narrowed.

He didn't say anything.

Sam noticed.

"What?" Sam asked.

Toby shook his head slightly.

Sam frowned. "What did you see?"

"Nothing," Toby said too quickly.

I glanced over. "Toby?"

He met my eyes, then looked away.

"I'm still sorting," he said.

Zara tilted her head, and she'd noticed too.

But Toby didn't offer the note; he slipped it into his pocket instead.

That alone would've been strange, but Toby wasn't the kind of person who hid things.

Unless he thought they needed to be handled carefully.

We packed up when the bell rang again, stuffing the notes into my bag and Zara's tote like we were clearing debris after a storm.

The afternoon dragged.

By the time school ended, my head felt full of paper.

Sam walked home beside me, unusually silent.

Toby lagged, staring at the ground like it might whisper answers.

Halfway down the path, he sped up and grabbed Sam's sleeve.

"Sam," he said urgently.

"What?"

"Not here," Toby said, glancing around.

They fell back, and I kept walking, pretending not to notice when we got home, I dumped the bag on my bed.

Notes spilled out again. I didn't read them. I couldn't.

I lay back and stared at the ceiling, the glow-in-the-dark stars feeling suddenly childish and comforting at the same time.

This wasn't fun anymore. This wasn't clever. This was heavy.

Later, when Sam and Toby came into the room, they were whispering fiercely.

Toby shut the door behind them.

"Okay," Sam said. "Say it again."

Toby took the green note from his pocket.

Sam's eyes widened.

"Green?"

"Yes."

Sam swallowed. "Like *green*, green?"

"Yes."

"That's new."

"I know."

Toby smoothed the paper flat on the desk.

"Only one person in the entire school uses green paper," he said quietly.

Sam stared.

"You're sure?"

Toby nodded. "Obsessively sure."

"Who?"

Toby hesitated.

"Say it," Sam said.

"Eli Turner," Toby whispered.

Sam's face drained of colour.

Eli Turner.

Year Five.

Always quiet, always polite, always helpful, and always wearing green.

Green hoodie, green socks, green pencil case. Even his water bottle was green.

"Eli wouldn't—" Sam began.

"He loves systems," Toby said. "He loves patterns. He loves being needed."

Sam sank onto the bed.

"And" Toby added, "he sits near the lockers. Every day."

Sam closed his eyes.

"He helped me once," Sam said softly. "With my timetable."

Toby nodded. "He helped me organise my space facts."

They sat in silence for a long moment.

"We can't just say it," Sam said finally.

"I know," Toby replied. "That's why I didn't tell Leo."

Sam looked up. "You think it's him?"

"I think," Toby said carefully, "he might be the inside person."

"Or" Sam said, "he might be being used."

"Either way," Toby said, "the green matters."

Sam nodded slowly.

"We need to be sure."

"Yes."

"And we need to tell Leo."

"Yes," Toby agreed. "But not yet."

Sam took a breath.

"Tomorrow," he said. "We watch Eli."

Toby nodded.

"Quietly."

"Quietly."

Across the room, I turned onto my side, pretending to sleep.

I'd heard everything.

Not because they were loud.

Because secrets don't stay secret when they're heavy enough.

I didn't say anything.

Not for the first time since this started, the noise was thinning.

And somewhere beneath the avalanche of notes, something solid was emerging.

Green.

And suddenly, the cost of secrecy felt sharper than ever.

Because knowing meant choosing what to do next.

And I wasn't sure I was ready for that choice.

CHAPTER 25

Confrontation

There are moments when everyone looks at you and you realise, too late, that something has already been decided.

That's how the meeting started.

We were back behind the gym, our unofficial headquarters, except this time no one was pacing, no one was joking, and no one was pretending this was just another clever problem to solve. The air felt tight, like it was being held in by everyone's ribs.

Sam stood with his hands shoved deep into his pockets.

Toby stood next to him, helmet under his arm, jaw set.

Zara didn't open her notebook.

Mia sat on the low concrete ledge, knees drawn up, watching me.

I knew before anyone spoke.

"Say it," I said.

Sam swallowed. "We think we know who the inside person is."

Zara nodded once. "Sam's theory holds."

My stomach flipped. "Who?"

Toby answered quietly. "Eli Turner."

The name landed heavier than I expected.

Eli Turner.

Green hoodie.

Green pencils.

Green everything.

Quiet voice.

Careful movements.

The kid who always raised his hand halfway, like he wasn't sure he deserved the full height.

He was a year behind me and much smaller in size than I was.

"That makes little sense," I said automatically. "He wouldn't—"

"He didn't start it," Sam blurted. "We don't think that."

"But he's involved," Zara added. "Or being used."

Mia frowned. "Why him?"

"Green paper," Toby said. "Distinct fold. Same pressure pattern as some of the earlier notes."

Zara finally opened her notebook and turned it so we could see. She'd drawn a timeline. Green had appeared once, then vanished. Now it was back.

"Eli's been close enough to your locker every day," Zara continued. "And he has access without raising suspicion."

"Because he's quiet," Mia said.

"And because no one watches the quiet ones," Sam added.

I rubbed my face.

"What now?" I asked.

Zara closed the notebook. "Now you talk to him."

My head snapped up. "Me?"

"Yes," she said simply.

"Why me?"

"Because you're at the centre of this and because he won't talk to anyone else," Zara replied.

Mia stood. "I'll come with you."

"No," Zara said immediately.

Mia stiffened. "Why not?"

"Because," Zara said gently, "this has to feel safe."

I laughed without humour. "Safe?"

Zara met my eyes. "As safe as it can be."

Sam stepped forward. "Leo, you need to put on your big-boy pants."

I stared at him. "Did you just say that to me?"

"Yes," Sam said. "Because this isn't about clever plans anymore. It's about answers."

"And," Toby added softly, "asking what he wants."

That part stuck.

Not *what he's done.*

What he *wants.*

I exhaled slowly.

"Fine," I said. "I'll talk to him."

Mia reached out and squeezed my hand once. "We're right here."

I nodded and went looking for Eli, and I found him sitting alone under the jacaranda tree near the fence, picking at the grass. His backpack was beside him, green straps looped neatly together. Of course.

I walked toward him, heart pounding so loud I was sure he could hear it.

He looked up when my shadow crossed him.

"Oh," he said. "Hi, Leo."

His voice cracked slightly.

"Hi," I said, stopping a few steps away. "Can I sit?"

He hesitated, then nodded. "Yeah."

For a moment, we just existed. The noise of the playground faded into something distant and blurry.

"I'm not in trouble, am I?" Eli asked suddenly.

The question hit harder than anything else.

"No," I said quickly. "No. This isn't about trouble."

He relaxed a fraction.

I chose my words carefully.

"Eli, I need to ask you something. And I need you to be honest."

He nodded. "I am honest."

"I know," I said, and I meant it.

"Have you been putting notes in my locker?"

His fingers stilled.

"No," he said immediately.

Too immediately not a lie, more like a reflex.

I didn't push yet.

"Okay," I said. "Then let me ask it differently."

He looked up at me, wary.

"Have you been given notes to pass on?"

His jaw tightened, and silence stretched.

I noticed how much bigger I was than him, how my knees rose higher, and how my voice carried more weight just by existing, and I hated that.

"Eli," I said softly, "I'm not here to accuse you. I'm here because things have gotten messy."

He glanced around, eyes flicking toward the lockers.

"People are scared," I continued. "I'm scared. And I think you might be too. These notes made the kids nervous."

His eyes flicked back to mine.

I saw it then, not guilt but fear.

"I don't want to be a bully," I said quickly. "And I don't want you to think I am."

"You're not," he said too fast.

"Then help me understand," I said. "Please."

His shoulders slumped.

"I didn't want this," he whispered.

My heart sank. "Did you help her?"

He flinched. "You know."

I nodded. "We figured it out."

He stared at the ground.

"She's my mum," he said finally.

The words were quiet, but they landed like something heavy dropped from a height.

"The Watcher," I said.

He nodded.

"She watches the school," he said quickly now, like he'd rehearsed this explanation in his head a hundred times. "But not like you think. She doesn't mean it in a scary way. She just wants to make sure my sister is okay. She always has."

I swallowed. "And the notes?"

Eli shook his head immediately. Hard.

"They weren't meant to scare anyone," he said. "They were never supposed to."

I blinked. "Then what were they?"

He hesitated, cheeks flushing red, his ears turning the same colour.

"They were love notes," he said quietly.

I stared at him. "Love notes?"

"For my sister to rewrite and place in different places so you notice the notes and maybe her," he rushed on.

My chest tightened.

"Your sister," I said.

"Abby," he nodded. "She's in Year Three."

That name settled differently than I expected.

"She has a crush on you," Eli said, barely above a whisper. "She thinks you're really kind. And smart. And cute."

My brain stumbled over that word.

Cute.

"She's really shy," he continued. "She gets scared easily. Mum worries about her all the time. About everyone, really. She thinks schools are dangerous places where kids get hurt with no one noticing."

My stomach dropped.

"So, the notes—" I began.

"—were supposed to be reassurance," Eli said quickly. "Like proof. Mum said if Abby rewrote the notes, left them for you to find and then saw that you were thoughtful, and gentle, and noticed things too, she'd feel less afraid. Like the world isn't as bad as she thinks."

I exhaled slowly.

"She thought," Eli went on, voice shaking now, "that if Abby believed someone good was watching out for things, she'd feel braver. That's why some notes talk about paying attention. About being careful."

"The warnings," I said quietly.

He nodded. "They weren't warnings to *you*. They were reminders. To me. To Abby. Mum thought they sounded comforting."

I closed my eyes.

Comfort written in the wrong language had turned into fear.

"Mum made me write some of them," Eli said. "The nicer ones. The ones about kindness. Sometimes she wrote them herself and asked me to pass them on to Abby. She said it was important that Abby felt hopeful."

"And the different colours?" I asked.

"Green was for Abby," he said softly. "Her favourite and mine. She said green felt safe."

Green.

"I didn't think it would turn into this," Eli whispered. "I didn't think people would get scared. Or that you'd get all those notes. Mum didn't either."

I opened my eyes.

This wasn't a mastermind; this wasn't a villain; this was fear wearing the wrong costume.

"Eli," I said carefully, "do you understand why this went wrong?"

He nodded hard. "Yes."

"Do you understand why it has to stop?"

"Yes," he said immediately this time.

"I'm going to tell the others," I said. "Not to get you into trouble. To fix this."

His head snapped up. "Will Abby get into trouble?"

"No," I said firmly. "None of this is her fault."

"And me?"

"You're not a bad person either," I said.

He nodded.

"Does this mean you like Abby?"

Oh boy, I thought to myself.

"Eli, Abby is probably a very, very nice little girl, but I am so much, I mean, so much older than she is, I do not think it will work out between us."

"So, what do I tell Abby? She is going to cry when I tell her you do not like her."

"No, wait. Do not tell her that. Just say you spoke with me about the notes and that I will speak with her by the end of the week. Deal?"

Eli thought for a moment, nodded, and just said: "Deal," and walked towards the playground.

When I walked back to the group, every step felt heavier than the last.

Mia searched my face, Zara straightened and Sam held his breath, and Toby asked: "What did he say?"

I had no choice. I needed to say it. Let it come out and see what happens. I mean, what is the worst that could happen?

"Eli admitted the notes were from the Watcher, who is his mother, and that the notes were for his little sister Abby to rewrite and place in different places for me to find."

The gang just looked at me and said nothing.

"The notes were some kind of joke?" Mia asked.

"No, not exactly," I answered.

"If not a joke, then what were they? I don't understand," remarked Zara.

"They were... encouragement. For his little sister to express herself."

Silence.

Mia spoke first, voice tight but steady. "What kind of encouragement?"

What can I say I did exactly what Sam said that I needed to do: put on my 'big boy pants'.

"They were supposed to be love notes to me from Abby, and I guess they came from love that did not know when to stop."

The faces. You should have seen their faces.

Mia, Zara, Sam, and Toby.

Faces of stone — that is what they looked like when they heard my explanation and then...

The silence was thick, punctuated only by the scratch of Toby scratching his head. That silence, however, was about to be obliterated by a single, hilarious revelation.

Then the dam broke. Zara was the first, letting out a sharp, surprised yelp she tried to turn into a cough. Sam immediately slapped his hand over his mouth, his shoulders shaking with silent, desperate laughter. "Dude, you're the school's new heartthrob!" he wheezed.

"Someone has a crush on you! That's next-level fame!" Toby, wiping a tear from his eye, contributed: "I bet you now cherish the notes. You should totally ask her out. Imagine the power! You could rule the smaller kids!"

Mia leaned back dramatically, a playful yet utterly mocking pout on her face.

Her laughter was the loudest.

"Oh, my gosh, Leo! How can I possibly compete? What am I to do now?" She declared, fanning herself. "It's the ultimate betrayal! I thought *I* was the only one allowed to obsessively stalk you... I mean, study with you! Now I have competition for your affection from someone who probably still thinks cooties are real! You better tell your little admirer that this level of sophistication requires a two-year age gap minimum."

The sight of my flustered face and the sheer, unexpected comedy of the situation sent them all into a final paroxysm of howling laughter, proving that even the most serious mysteries can be completely derailed by a tiny, love-struck girl and a piece of paper.

CHAPTER 26

The Secret Is Out

The secret did not tiptoe out; it sprinted. By Monday morning, I was no longer Leo Marshall, a regular kid from locker 217 who sometimes jammed and a brother who talked too much about space.

I was Leo Marshall, the *Cutest.*

I did not ask for this title; I did not approve it, but it arrived anyway.

It started with Ben calling out, "Oi, Cute Guy," across the oval, which made everyone laugh except me, because I tripped over absolutely nothing and almost face-planted into the grass.

Then came the boys, and they were relentless.

"Careful, Leo," one said as I opened my lunchbox. "You might attract a crowd."

"Sign my shoe," another added. "I want proof I knew you *before* you were cute."

Sam was the worst.

He walked past me at recess, sighed dramatically, and said, "Must be hard being everyone's emotional support crush."

I told him to stop.

He told me to embrace my destiny.

The girls were different.

Not obvious, just worse.

Smiles that lasted half a second too long. Sitting slightly closer than necessary. Whispering that stopped when I turned my head.

Mia handled it with impressive maturity.

By which I mean she laughed every single time someone called me cute and said, "Told you," like this had always been obvious and I'd just been slow.

I wanted the ground to swallow me.

But this is important; I was also a bit proud.

Not proud-proud, just... secretly proud.

I stood a little taller.

Fixed my hair in the library's reflection window. Considered briefly whether my hoodie colour mattered.

(It did not. I still wore the same one.)

The Watcher, Eli's mum, had stopped coming to the path. The notes had stopped completely. The avalanche had melted into stories, then rumours, then legends.

By the end of the week, the mystery had become a myth.

And myths always get edited.

By Friday, the story was that I'd solved everything single-handedly while staring meaningfully into the distance.

This version was incorrect, but I gave up trying to correct it.

I had told Eli that I would talk to Abby, so asked him to meet me after school near the basketball courts and to bring Abby.

He arrived early, as always, Abby trailing behind him like a cautious moon orbiting a very green planet. She wore a green jacket, green sneakers, and a headband that looked like it had been chosen with great seriousness.

She stopped when she saw me.

Completely.

Like someone had pressed pause.

"Oh," she said.

I smiled.

This was it.

The moment I had been slightly, terribly dreading.

"Hi, Abby," I said.

Her face turned pink, not red, but pink. Like someone had gently switched on a light behind her cheeks.

"H-hi," she said.

Eli cleared his throat. "I'll... uh... stand over there."

He retreated to a bench and immediately pretended to be very interested in his shoelaces.

Abby stared at me, and I stared back, and this was awkward, so I went first.

"So," I said, "I heard you like video games."

Her eyes widened. "You know about *Galactic Quest*?"

Sam would have loved her instantly.

"I do," I said. "I'm not great at it."

"That's okay," she blurted. "I'm really good. I can help."

I nodded seriously. "I appreciate that."

She shifted her weight from foot to foot.

"I, um," she said, "my brother said you're very nice."

I glanced at Eli, who was now pretending to tie his shoe for the third time.

"I try," I said.

Abby took a deep breath.

"I like you," she announced.

There it was. Clear, brave, and honest.

I felt my chest tighten in a way that wasn't panic. Just responsibility.

"That's really kind," I said carefully. "And I'm really glad you told me."

Her shoulders relaxed a little.

"I was thinking," I continued, "maybe after school sometimes we could play a game together. Like not a scary one. Just fun."

Her face lit up.

"Like a date?" she asked hopefully.

I hesitated.

Just for a second.

Then I said, "Like hanging out."

She nodded enthusiastically. "Yes. A hanging-out date."

That seemed close enough.

She grinned so hard I thought her face might crack.

"I'm telling Mum," she said.

"Okay," I replied, slightly terrified but committed now.

Eli walked back over.

"Is she okay?" he asked.

"She's great," I said.

Abby waved at me three times as they left.

Not once, not twice, but three times.

Sam appeared immediately as if by magic.

"Well?" he demanded.

"I survived," I said.

"And?" Mia asked, appearing on my other side.

"And," I said, "I might be playing video games with a Year Three girl who thinks it's a date."

Mia burst out laughing.

Zara shook her head. "You're doomed."

I watched Abby skip toward the gate, Eli following like a relieved satellite.

The mystery was solved.

The notes were gone.

The Watcher was no longer watching.

But as I adjusted my backpack and felt three different people glance at me at once, I realised something important.

Being cute was complicated, awkward, and unexpected, and maybe just beginning.

I sighed.

Some mysteries end.

Others just change shape.

And judging by the way Sam was grinning at me like he knew something I didn't—
This one definitely wasn't over yet.

About the Author

José F. Nodar

Flung into one of life's biggest challenges at just eleven, José's story began in Havana, Cuba. The Cuban Revolution forced him onto a plane alone, landing him at an orphanage in a small Georgia town called Washington. Reuniting with his parents wouldn't happen until he was eighteen, a high school graduate in Atlanta.

Business Administration became his focus at Georgia State University. From there, he navigated the world of finance, first at the First National Bank of Atlanta (now Wells Fargo) and later as a project manager in financial consulting. These roles took him across the United States, Europe, and even Australia.

It was in Camden, New South Wales, Australia, that a spark ignited José's creative side. A writers' group became the launching pad for his debut novel, and soon, his mind birthed Danny Monk, his first major character.

But José's life isn't all about writing. When he's not crafting captivating stories, you might find him at the local mall, observing the world and gathering inspiration for future characters. Away from his computer, he dives into books or enjoys long strolls around Spring Farm.

Copyright © 2026 by José F. Nodar

Other books by José F. Nodar

English

Books, Pens & Larceny

Mending Hearts at Crystal Cove

A Love Finally Spoken

The Legacy Compass

The Universe Between Us

The Time Bus

SEX

The Compass Legacy

The Teacher's Assistant

Somewhere in Time

The Northport Coffee Group

Stories to Share with My Partner Book 1

Stories to Share with My Partner Book 2

Stories to Share with My Partner Book 3

Stories to Share with My Partner Book 4

Stories to Share with My Partner Book 5

Stories to Share with My Partner Book 6

Stories to Share with My Partner Book 7

Stories to Share with My Partner Book 8

Stories to Share with My Partner Book 9

Stories to Share with My Partner Book 10

Locker 217

Stories to Share with My Partner Book 11

Spanish

- Cuentos Para Compartir con Mi Pareja Libro 1
- Cuentos Para Compartir con Mi Pareja Libro 2
- Cuentos Para Compartir con Mi Pareja Libro 3
- Libros, Bolígrafos y Hurto
- Reparando Corazones en Crystal Cove
- Un Amor Finalmente Declarado
- El Autobús del Tiempo